Doc-in a-Box

A Novel

Robert A. Burton

SOHO

Copyright © 1991 by Robert A. Burton
All rights reserved. Published by
Soho Press, Inc.
1 Union Square
New York, NY 10003

Library of Congress Cataloging-in-Publication Data
Burton, Robert Alan, 1941–
Doc-in-a-box ; a novel / by Robert A. Burton.
p. cm.
ISBN 0-939149-47-8
I. Title.
PS3552.U7824D6   1991
813′.54—dc20   90-10315
                                                            CIP

Manufactured in the United States
First Edition

To Adrianne and my parents; my family.

Doc-in a-Box

It had been a day of breasts and chins, mostly second opinions and idle queries. Window shopping, he would tell Elizabeth over dinner. Webb opened his bottom desk drawer; there was a pint of Jack Daniel's and a silver shot glass. He deliberated, then slid the drawer shut. He leaned back in his chair and dreamed of a vacation in a land without mirrors.

Webb had hoped to make a practice of reconstruction work, and had taken additional training in cleft palates and craniofacial anomalies. But it was hard getting started. His university clinic service paid nothing. After six years in practice, vanity remained his bread and butter.

He heard the front door to his office suite open—Mrs. Ramirez, the cleaning lady. She had been a shopkeeper in San Salvador. She was usually slightly apologetic, calling him "Doctor" in a tone of voice that suggested she was addressing a priest. She embarrassed Webb, made him want to seem more than he knew he was.

He waited for the sound of the vacuum cleaner in the waiting room. Instead Mrs. Ramirez was talking to someone else, at first quietly, then more heatedly. Then she appeared in front of him in his consultation room. Alongside her was a street tough of about nineteen. The boy was bent forward at the waist; he held a blue denim jacket tightly against his blood-soaked thigh. On his belt was a Pac Bell beeper.

"He's my only boy," she explained. "We didn't know where to go."

"County Hospital's only a few minutes away. Here, I'll give you cab money."

The boy shook his head. He stared at Webb, his eyes hard, yet pleading. When he lifted up the bloody jacket to reposition it, Webb saw the small hole.

His mother came forward, her hands clasped in front of her. "He's good. It was an accident. Please."

"What happened?" Webb said to him.

"Come on, let's go," the boy said to his mother.

"No. Dr. Smith will help you." It was that inflection in her voice: "Doctor."

"I can't. It's against the law."

"They'll send him to jail. And it wasn't his fault."

"I'm sorry. It just isn't possible."

"Please," the woman said. "No one will know."

"Come on," the boy said. "Don't beg. Besides, he ain't worth shit." He turned and walked back into the waiting room.

Life had become a parade of millimeters, his office the

Tiffany of angles and curves, nips and tucks. He was a self-ordained master of the superficial.

"I'm really sorry," Webb said. "You know that I'd like to, but . . ."

Mrs. Ramirez started out of his consultation room, joining her son who was waiting with the front door open. Her shoulders were hunched in defeat. Webb hated to think of the expression on her face. Well, so what. He was what he was, a plastic surgeon in tinseltown, a touch-up artist, a soap-opera doctor with no reasonable claim to authenticity. He heard the front door close.

And for no reason at all, he found himself running down the hall, catching the two of them at the elevator. "You promise you won't tell anyone," he said to the boy.

The son nodded.

"You absolutely promise?"

"My word is my life."

The bullet was lodged in the quadriceps muscle. It took only a few minutes to remove. Mrs. Ramirez packed up the surgical supplies, then washed down the floors until the room was spotless. She walked over to Webb, and kissed him on the cheek. Her eyes were filled with tears. Moments later she was vacuuming the waiting room, and the boy was off the treatment table, stiffly sliding on his blood-soaked pants.

"Here, wear these." Webb handed him a green operating room scrub suit, after first being sure it was not labeled.

The boy put on the scrub suit, then fastened his beeper at the waist. It was the same model that Webb wore. After dressing, the boy came into Webb's consultation room, carrying his bloody clothes under his arm. He walked around the desk to where Webb was sitting, and dropped a small vial of white powder on the desk.

"It's top grade. For you and your wife." He motioned to the picture of Elizabeth on Webb's credenza. Beyond the window the sun was ducking behind the Union Bank.

"No." Webb pushed the vial back across the desk.

"No one does nothing for me for free. You take it." He reached around the desk and opened Webb's bottom drawer, then ceremoniously closed it.

Three weeks later, caught in a drug bust, the boy sang like an opera star. Within five minutes they had Webb's address. And where to look for the cocaine.

Webb glanced at the sheet of paper neatly tacked to the bulletin board outside the hearing room. "Webb Smith, M.D." rose off the page as though it were the only name. He swallowed and quickly looked away, as though turning away might undo it, maybe even remove him from the list. He stepped to the other side of the corridor and took a seat on a long wooden bench next to a low enamel drinking fountain and across from an arched window. It was early spring; a cherry tree just beyond the window was beginning to blossom. A gust of wind carried away some of the petals.

After the hearing, the results would be compiled in a bulletin sent to all the medical agencies in the state. Doctors, nurses, hospital administrators, the university surgical departments—everyone would know the details. But they already knew; he had made the front page of the L.A. *Times*.

Two other doctors shared the bench. He recognized neither. One was dressed in a conservative gray worsted suit, wore monogrammed cuff links, and looked like a businessman waiting while the board of directors voted on his promotion. He was nervous, fidgeted, drank coffee from a paper cup, and glanced at the morning paper.

To Webb's left was a slight, bedraggled man who reeked of mouthwash. His face was flushed. He sat—elbows on knees, head bent forward—and said nothing. His shoes were dusty and scuffed; there was a hole in one blue sock. He saw Webb looking at him, laughed, and looked away.

Webb felt like talking, but there was nothing to say. This was not a time to invoke the camaraderie of being fellow physicians. Not when they were, in the eyes of their profession, scum.

The hearing was being held in a board room of the County Medical Society. Down the hall were the secretarial offices, women typing and chatting. Occasionally one of them would poke her head out into the corridor to get a look at the accused. Once these women had been his allies. They arranged for his health, malpractice, and dental insurance. They sent him brochures for continuing education events. They served him. This morning he had walked by them, face averted.

In olden days they drove the condemned through the streets, in open carts, in plain view. Now they made you wait in the long silent corridors of state buildings.

Webb ran his clammy hand along the varnished wood of the bench, leaving a thin damp trail of dread. His future would be determined in the hearing room. It was crazy; he had taken out a bullet, that was all. As for the cocaine, plenty of the doctors at the hospital bought coke from the charge nurse in come-and-go surgery. No one reported her. But because Mrs. Ramirez's son had syndicate connections, the district attorney's office was going to make an example of everyone involved.

"Do you think they will prosecute?" the grubby doctor asked. His face glistened with sweat; he was blinking rapidly.

"Hard to say." Webb could not imagine them actually sending him to prison. Yet it happened all the time. Prisons were filled with shrewd, educated men who had never dreamed that they would end up behind bars. "I suppose. But it's doubtful." His voice lacked conviction.

"I hope those bastards take into account all I've done. Twenty-eight years in practice should count for something."

"Sure," Webb said. The man was sincere but pathetic. Maybe the man's twenty-eight years were worth something, maybe they weren't. A quarter century ago he might have been a hard-working, journal-reading idealist. A friend of Webb's had run the recent L.A. marathon. At eighteen miles he was in first place; at twenty miles he dropped out with a shin splint. The next day the papers listed him as a DNF: Did Not Finish. The ill-kempt man would be a DNF. The rest of the race would be forgotten.

Webb kept his distance from the well-dressed doctor, not responding to the man's occasional glances in his direction. He was relieved when the medical society secretary appeared and led the man inside.

"He fucked his patients while they were under anesthesia," the disheveled doctor said. "Not very attractive." He shifted in his seat; there was the odor of mildew. "I hope they throw the book at him."

"Yeah," Webb said. The two men looked at each other, as if about to speak. The other rose abruptly, walked to the drinking fountain, took a handful of water and splashed it on his face. He wiped it with his coat sleeve. Then he half-heartedly began to clean his blackened fingernails, using an uncurled paper clip.

Webb remained on the bench and ran through his defense. He had made a mistake. But he hadn't done it to get free drugs. It wasn't at all like what the Ramirez boy had said.

The other man was called next. As he slipped into the hearing room, the secretary leaned down and told Webb that he might as well get some lunch; they wouldn't get to him until two o'clock at the earliest.

From his booth at a Hof Brau House across the street, Webb watched clusters of secretaries on their lunch break, smoking, drinking coffee, eating diet salads, and gossiping. Webb was envious. By the end of the day he could be without the solace of routine, unless being unemployed had its own rhythms.

He ordered another beer, shoving aside a barely touched pastrami on rye. The waitress took his empty glass, wiped the wet ring of condensation from his table, at the same time briefly looking at Webb with an expression he interpreted as pity. Though it was unrealistic, it did feel as if the whole world was aware of his offense.

What a fool he had been. "You must be wired for self-destruction," he could hear Elizabeth say. "What did you think you were proving?"

I wasn't proving anything, Webb had replied.

"Then you did it to see what you could lose."

An hour later she was packed and gone. A week later she was back. "It isn't this, it's everything that's gone before, Webb. One last try," she said, hanging her clothes in her closet. "But it means counseling, frank discussions about kids, concrete evidence that you are trying."

And he tried. He saw a therapist and tried to make changes. But in the weeks before the hearing, unable to sleep, he had begun drinking in the evenings. There was no final conversation. On the day of her departure, Elizabeth spent the afternoon cooking turkey with all the trimmings. She arranged a single setting, complete with flowers, and was gone before Webb arrived home from the office. Propped up on the vase was a note. Webb crumpled it into a ball and threw it in the garbage bag under the sink. Later he sorted through the turkey innards and sweet potato peelings and retrieved it. It said: I love you. Or: I loved you. There was a smear of cranberry on the message; either sentence was possible.

It was an amicable separation; legal expenses and a ruined practice left little to quibble over.

Webb felt the waitress staring at him. He looked over; she might have been considering him, or she could have been daydreaming. He smiled weakly and ordered another beer. She had nice legs; if he felt like it after the hearing, he might come back and buy her a drink. The waitress asked if he wanted his sandwich wrapped to go.

"I guess I'm dieting," Webb said, pushing the sandwich away.

"It's perfectly good; I made it myself. You could have it for dinner."

"Put it in the fridge. I'll be back for it at Happy Hour."

"You'll be back after work?" she asked. Her face seemed cautious but ready to smile.

"Yeah, after work. You can count on it."

Webb switched to whiskey to wash down the taste of his upcoming testimony. By the time two o'clock rolled around, oiled by three Jack Daniel's, Webb was inflamed, mad at himself, at the system, at the holier-than-thou doctors who would now sit in judgment. What right did the committee have to question him? After all, wasn't it a doctor's primary obligation to heal the sick and injured?

He took his seat in front of the half-circle of his colleagues. The room was stuffy; sun streamed through the closed windows. An old-fashioned steam radiator banged away in the corner of the room. It was getting warmer by the minute. A court reporter sat alongside Webb, taking notes. She periodically wiped her neck with a lavender-scented tissue. Webb felt lightheaded and short of breath; he wanted to loosen his tie. The eight physicians and Renshaw from the Board of Medical Quality Assurance stared at him, their expressions uniformly stern. Garbed for judgment, they wore elegantly tailored suits. Webb sat upright in his chair, carefully aligned his feet, folded his hands in his lap. He adjusted his tie more tightly, fingering the opening of his collar to check the fit. Beads of sweat gathered behind his knees. One ran down the back of his calf.

Charlie Picow, the head of orthopedic surgery at Good Hope, led the questioning. He and Webb shared adjacent lockers in the doctors' dressing room. Picow was particularly good with over-the-counter stocks and lumbar laminectomies. Webb had distrusted him from the time of their first introduction. Picow glad-handed as though he was campaigning for some undisclosed political office. Neurosurgeons at the hospital had told Webb that Picow operated on patients with MRI and CAT scans that were normal. Picow had become a self-proclaimed expert, claiming that he knew more than the scans revealed. He made the patients sign extensive waivers to protect himself from any potential litigation and called these surgeries "exploratory."

Webb fumed at the thought of Charlie Picow heading his investigation. The two men looked at each other. Webb nodded, trying to remain cordial. Picow was expressionless.

"We've gone over the charges," Picow began. "They're very serious. Mr. Renshaw informs me that you've violated enough statutes to make San Quentin." Picow glanced at a diminutive young man seated at the far end of the conference table. "However, we're willing to hear your side."

Charlie Picow's pompous delivery distracted and irritated Webb. He forgot the beginning of his prepared speech. He drew a blank, feeling only a vast drowsiness, a strange indifference. How could he be judged by men who took out perfectly good uteruses, normal discs, and shiny, healthy gallbladders? This meeting was just a formality, a going through the motions. He would humbly apologize, and they would let him go. At worst he would get a warning.

"We're waiting," Charlie Picow said.

The thick still air and the Jack Daniel's clotted his mind. He ran down the row of his interrogators, judging as he was being judged. He caught the eye of Roger Bean, a family practitioner who took his own calls seven days a week. Made *house* calls. He drove an old Chevrolet and lived in a modest section of West L.A. He was the old-style family doctor; he made the other doctors on the staff uneasy. They publicly proclaimed admiration for him, but felt privately that his example made them look bad.

When Webb started in practice, Bean had sent him patients. There had not been any referrals recently, but that could have been because Bean had no one to send. Or it could have meant that Bean had changed his opinion of Webb. He had no way of knowing. He looked closely, but he could not read Bean's expression.

He could ignore the opinion of Picow, whom he despised. But not Bean.

And maybe there really was more to what he had done than simply treating the injured. Maybe it was his way of getting back, letting out the anger that ate away at him. Fuck authority—the words constantly camped out at the tip of his tongue, poised to be uttered when someone irritated him. Maybe he did do it to show everyone, or if not everyone, at least himself and the Ramirezes, that he was bigger than petty laws. The system didn't give a damn about the little guy: people on welfare, the homeless, the sick poor.

He felt Bean staring at him, through him. There was nothing he could say. Picow droned on, accusing him of thinking just what he had been thinking, that he was above the law.

"Isn't that right, Dr. Smith?" Picow leaned forward, his chin resting in his hand. "Isn't that the real truth?"

Why should he apologize to *Picow?* The Jack Daniel's burned in Webb's brain. He said, "A fair number of the doctors at our illustrious Good Hope Hospital take drugs. We don't blow the whistle on them, or on a certain OR nurse who so kindly distributes the drugs, for a fee. Personally, I don't see any difference between not reporting her and not reporting a gunshot wound. Or someone who jacks up Medi-

1 3

Cal billings." Webb stared at Picow. "The boy was hurt and I took care of him. I realize that's against the law, but I did it. And I'm sorry. And, if pushed, I would probably do it again. Period. End of discussion."

It wasn't at all what he had planned on saying.

"For a price," Mr. Renshaw said. "A trade of services, as I understand it."

"That's not true."

"The police found the vial of cocaine in your desk drawer. With Ramirez's fingerprints on it."

"Well, that's not the way it happened." He wanted to explain about the expression on Mrs. Ramirez's face, but now he could see that the less he said the better. "Ramirez insisted I take the drugs." There were scattered laughs from the members of the panel. "It was not a fee."

"It's too bad. You did good work," Bean said. He turned toward Renshaw. "He was one of my favorite consultants, a good doctor. You might take that into consideration." He looked over at Webb. "I'm really sorry that you're here."

"Don't waste your pity," Picow said. "Mr. Renshaw, please proceed."

Renshaw stepped forward to stand between Webb and the panel. Webb was vaguely amused. His sentence would be meted out by a little man wearing a jacket with wide, outdated lapels.

"One year suspension of all medical privileges," Renshaw said.

The words were so precise that Webb had trouble fully grasping their implication. He wanted to smash the little man in his bureaucratic, smug face.

"You'll be called down to the district attorney's office to discuss the criminal charges."

"Criminal charges? You can't be serious."

Renshaw took his seat and shuffled some papers into his briefcase. He did not answer Webb.

"This was all prearranged, wasn't it? A setup." He could accuse them all he wanted. His career was over. Tomorrow Picow would be back strutting through the halls of the hospital, all the other pompous turd doctors would be back at their posts at Good Hope, and Renshaw would gleefully sign the papers putting Webb out of business. The realization finally dawned.

He'd been a fool. He needed a lawyer.

Webb did not remember walking to the door, or crossing the street to the nearest bar. He drank until closing time.

T. Edwin Butz was an advocate. His outfit was flawless, right down to his manicured nails. A red handkerchief flowered from his pin striped suit jacket. His shoes were shiny; the ribs of his socks rose in perfect verticals. Webb had tried to hire the best, which meant the worst. Butz was despicable. But he was a friend of several judges, and knew half the staff of the district attorney's office. Webb reminded himself that Butz was only a tool, a hired gun. But he found himself being overly solicitous, smiling and nodding when there was no reason. He would have to put up with Butz, and himself, and hope for the best.

They met in the basement of City Hall. Inspector Zachary Reynolds of the Los Angeles Police Department, Assistant District Attorney Malcolm Appleton, Butz, and Webb. Reynolds semi-reclined, his chair tilted to forty-five degrees, his head resting against a greasy basement window. Reynolds was tall, clean-cut, wore gray-tinted glasses and an open-necked polo shirt. He spoke quietly, as though addressing a child. Webb guessed that he used the same soft-spoken technique on everyone from accident victims to murderers. Appleton sat behind a gray metal desk, an imitation leather briefcase on the floor in the corner. There were a number of manila folders and yellow lined pads full of notes piled on the desk. Appleton sorted through the stack until he found Webb's file. He could have been a doctor, checking through the patient's past history for warning signs, risk factors, tendencies. He read in silence while Butz stood, arms folded, in front of the desk.

Webb tried to remain inconspicuous in a corner of the tiny room. He would have opted for invisibility, but that was not possible. It was his basement-level day of judgment.

Reynolds picked his nails and worked out a scuff in his shoes. Appleton tapped his pencil on the desk in a constant rhythm, as he mulled over the information. Butz remained motionless. A fly landed on Webb's computer printout. Without looking, Appleton brushed it away. The fly landed on the telephone. It moved across the dial, walked across the desk, and was smacked to a black smudge by Reynolds's fist. "I hate flies," Reynolds said.

On the day of judgment, will there be background music and little cakes for the waiting? Webb envisioned long lines of people standing in the hot sun, peering over the edge of the precarious platform on which they stood in the sky, fearful of falling. Webb wiped his hands on his gray slacks.

"Okay," Appleton said finally. "Tell me why we shouldn't lock up the good Dr. Smith." He pointed his pencil at Butz. "And make it quick." Before Butz could begin, Appleton swiveled around in his chair, presenting the back of his head to Butz. He looked out the basement window at a paddy wagon unloading a group of shackled prisoners. The men walked into the building, heads down, their legs chained together. A metal door slammed behind them. "Give me your best shot," he said, addressing the window.

"Let's start with his background." Butz pulled some papers from his briefcase and began to recite Webb's past. Webb listened attentively, interested in hearing how his life might sound to someone else. But there was a great distance between the facts, which were correct, and his own sense of himself. It sounded like someone else's life. Butz focused on Webb's days as a paramedic and ambulance driver. "Summers, nights, weekends, from the time he was a high school senior. Blood and guts, and no glory. Except for the L.A. Medal of Honor for the time he saved the boy's life in the Watts riot." Butz emphasized the word *honor*, then started describing how he had earned it. Webb had given him the information. In the privacy of Butz's office it had seemed like a good approach. Now, it seemed extraneous. But Butz was undaunted. He went over the events leading up to the award in painstaking detail as though this single act of heroism could outweigh subsequent crimes.

Then Butz went through Webb's humble background, describing the death of his parents in a car accident when Webb was only fifteen, his residence with a reluctant, elderly aunt until he went away to college on a partial scholarship. Butz painted a picture of economic struggle and single-minded purposefulness. Butz lingered on words like *dedication* and *sacrifice*. He suggested a depth of motivation, a clarity of intent, that, were Webb not so nervous, would have made him laugh. The selected facts presented in Butz's voice seemed to qualify Webb for sainthood. Butz was a pro.

Webb's moment of optimism was not justified.

"You make me sick," Reynolds said, pointing his finger at Butz. "Every day it's someone different. Pimps, hookers, pushers, you name it, you come in here with a canned sob story for the whole lot of them. You must really take us for fools."

Appleton spun around in his chair. "Excuses are bullshit. You do what you have to do, but you take the responsibility. If I sat here all day and tried to assess motivation, we'd need a hundred policemen assigned to investigate every crime. We'd have psychiatrists searching under every rock, to see if the kid was abused, abandoned, tortured, humiliated, in any way insulted. And everyone would turn up with reasons, excuses.

"The law is the law, pure and simple. You break it, you pay. I've heard enough," Appleton concluded. "Close the door on your way out. We'll see you in court tomorrow at 9:00 A.M."

Butz hurried off to another appointment. Webb had no place special to go. His mouth and throat were dry. He stopped at the snack shop on the first floor of the courthouse and bought a Pepsi. The cashier wore dark glasses and stared vacantly as he felt the coins to count them. After handing Webb his change, the man ran his hands over the rows of candy bars, straightening them. He rearranged a stack of licorice sticks. Webb watched in fascination. A sign over the cash register stated that the city hired the handicapped.

Across the hall, above the main entrance was a bas-relief of the scales of justice. Commit a crime and hire a lawyer—the more money, the better the lawyer. Go blind and there is no one to present your case, no justice. The cashier could not see the concrete scales carved into eternal balance. Whatever sentence he received, Webb knew it could never equal the man's sentence to sightlessness. And what did he deserve? He had been blessed with good health, a decent brain, a lovely wife, a promising career. He had already had more than his share. In his heart he knew he was entitled to nothing. But he hoped for leniency. What good would it do to send him to jail?

He had a dull, irritating headache. He searched his pockets for a Valium. Nothing. He was running on empty.

The blind man took a quarter from an old woman, and without looking, dropped it in the correct slot in the cash register. Webb walked away.

The entrance to the building was swarming. Crowds gathered in front of the doors to each of the municipal courtrooms. There was a peculiar excitement; clusters of people talked heatedly among themselves. Some talked to themselves. Others sat on benches and stared at the old, mottled, gray marble floors.

Webb wandered over to the nearest courtroom. Through the glass in the top half of the doors Webb could see a prisoner, dressed in an orange jump suit, standing in front of the judge. Webb opened a door and stood at the back of the room. The prisoner was taken away. A slight black man in faded clothes and a dirty tan rain hat came forward. He took off his hat, held it behind him as he approached the judge. His lawyer stood at his side while the judge reviewed some documents. The court reporter joked with the bailiff, trading gossip. The judge looked up but did not speak. He scanned the courtroom, drummed his fingers on the papers, looked down at the black man.

"I could send you to jail, or I could let you go." The judge stopped and stared at the accused.

Webb turned and left the room before he could hear the

decision. Submitting to fate was bad enough; worse yet was the idea that any man could have so much control over another man's life.

His car was parked three blocks away, in an alley. A half dozen Latino kids were gathered in a doorway just opposite the car. Another was casually sitting on the hood. For a split second Webb considered walking in the other direction. Don't be ridiculous, he told himself.

He began to unlock the car door. "Sorry," he said to the boy draped over his hood, "I've got to take your bench away."

The boy looked at him, then at his friends. A really big kid stepped out of the doorway, paused, gave Webb the once-over, and shook his head. The boy stepped away from the MG. "No problema. Just remember to drive safely."

Webb started the motor, nodded at the group, and eased out into the alleyway.

He turned right onto the main thoroughfare. There was a squeal of wheels as an old Chevy swerved to avoid him. Webb strained to see the driver. He could see nothing but a dark figure gunning his way through the heavy rush hour traffic.

The MG tended to overheat; the temperature gauge hovered at the edge of the red bar. Webb turned off the radio and again mulled over the possibilities. But with each additional block between himself and the Hall of Justice, the impact of the recent meeting diminished. When he arrived in Venice, it seemed as if he had driven from another state. Whatever he had done, whatever might happen to him was linked to downtown L.A. In Venice was sun, sand, and anonymity.

For a moment he enjoyed the pleasure of imagining that he was invisible, that crossing the town line granted him immunity.

He pulled on a sweater and walked down to the beach. It was nearly dusk. Occasional joggers passed, some running on concrete, others on the sand. Webb walked out to the surf's edge.

Butz had been eloquent. Whether or not Appleton and Reynolds had listened, Butz had made him into a minor hero. "He did it out of the urge to help." Those were Butz's words. Perhaps Appleton and Reynolds would discuss the case with their wives. Webb tried to imagine the women telling them to go easy on him, a doctor, not a criminal.

Butz was right. He had put in years of struggle, paid his dues. What he had not said about Webb was that he found it easier to work for a distant prize, no matter how difficult to win, than to live the comfortable life he had attained. Webb was reminded of Walter Overstreet, a doctor friend who bought a new suit every year and put it in the back of his closet, choosing instead to wear shabby, frayed ones. Webb had kidded him, asking why he never wore the new suits. Walter always answered that they were too good to be worn. He was waiting for the right occasion. Webb wondered if he, too, had simply been unable to enjoy what he had earned.

He stood at the water's edge, the sky softly darkening, the stars hovering on the edge of vision. Maybe the upcoming punishment would settle his debts. He had the feeling that it was not too late. A flock of sea gulls flew overhead, squawking.

Webb waited by himself, impatiently. It was already 9:15. Alone, he felt naked, vulnerable. Butz came jogging down the hall just as the door opened and Reynolds motioned Webb inside. "Sorry I was late," he whispered to Webb, taking a neatly folded handkerchief and wiping his forehead and upper lip. "But you'll be glad I was."

Appleton wore the same outfit as yesterday, right down to the same scuffed shoes. He looked even more uncomfortable.

"Is this your doing?" Reynolds said to Butz. He shook a piece of paper at him.

"What are you accusing me of?" Butz asked. "My responsibility is to my client."

"What a joke this job is. Well, Dr. Smith, this is your lucky day. You have just won the prison lottery."

"Excuse me?" Webb said. He wanted to reach out and grab the paper from Reynolds's hand. Instead he waited politely.

"Dr. Smith, do you want to strike a deal?" Appleton said. His voice shook and his face and neck were red.

"What are you offering?"

"Community service instead of the can."

"With no charges on the record. And a written guarantee that his license will be reinstated when his period of suspension is over," Butz insisted.

Reynolds and Appleton put their heads together and whispered for a few moments. "No guarantees. One hundred hours, not a second less. And the ten thousand that he has in the bank."

Butz turned to Webb, his back to the two men. "Take it,"

he whispered. Before Webb could answer, Butz turned back to Appleton.

"Eight thousand. There are costs."

"You're a real beauty."

Butz shrugged.

Appleton looked down at his papers. "It'll be roadwork. Rock-breaking, something physical to get you back into shape."

"You sure he couldn't work in a clinic, do something useful? No need to be vindictive, just because the prisons are overcrowded."

"No clinic. Roadwork. Take it or leave it. Albert Schweitzer can pick up loose papers with a stick. Clean up under the freeways. Pick up trash."

"Thank you," Webb said.

"Don't thank me," Appleton said. "I'd have your ass in jail. But it's a bad week." He held up the sheet of paper. "Word from Superior Court is that the jails are jammed full. Don't thank me, thank Jailhouse Butz. Johnny-on-the-spot. For a price."

Before leaving Butz made sure he got the deal in writing.

"**T**reat you to lunch," Webb said, once they were out in the corridor. But Butz was looking over Webb's shoulder.

"Excuse me a moment." He stepped around Webb. "How're you doing?" he asked, shaking hands with another lawyer.

"Rape case. Cut and dried. A real scumbag. Three priors. But the judge owes me one. I'll get him six months suspended." He laughed. "And you?"

"Nothing special. A doctor without a license." Butz mumbled something that Webb could not make out.

Returning to Webb, Butz said, "It'll be another thousand. Unforeseen expenses."

"I'll mail you a check," Webb promised.

"Fine." Butz offered his hand. "Any time I can be of service."

Webb sat in the back row of the van. A deputy sheriff in a green uniform explained the procedure as he drove. Two hours work, fifteen minutes break, half hour for lunch. They could bring a thermos of coffee and a lunch pail. The man droned on about punctuality, threatened them with extra time for laying down on the job. Cars passed the van, people stared in, trying to look at the faces of the men inside. Webb watched the people, knowing they were wondering what it felt like to be inside, to be labeled a criminal.

The van pulled off the freeway into an underpass, parked in a vast concrete expanse under the rumbling traffic. The embankment cast a rectangular shadow over broken asphalt. The Los Angeles River had once flowed here; now this basin was an unofficial dump site for garbage launched from passing cars. Garbage was everywhere, everything imaginable: a rotting remnant of hot dog, blood-splattered old shoes, a shredding mattress, a mangled baby carriage without wheels. Refuse came sliding down the steep incline beneath the overpass to the sound of shattering glass.

"Gentlemen, the place is to be spotless by afternoon." The deputy handed Webb a pole with a metal spike fixed at its end, then a thick heavily-spotted burlap bag. Webb slung the bag over his shoulder, fixed the stick in his hand, and set forth.

He was grateful that the day was overcast and cool. The odor of rodents, decay, dirt, and dust would have been overwhelming in the heat. He worked his way through the debris, picking up papers and manageable bits of trash. The others were working on abandoned mattresses, box springs, couches, and much that was not easily identifiable. Two men lifted up a tractor tire and threw it into a debris box.

One of them walked over to Webb. "You don't think you could help us with the heavier stuff, do you?" Then he broke into a broad smile.

A distant memory surfaced. Webb saw shreds of flesh hanging like strips of bacon. The man had been in a gang fight; two men had dragged him face down along a roll of barbed wire fencing. It had been a miracle that the facial nerve had regenerated, that the skin had not sloughed. Webb had finished his rotation as chief resident before the keloids started to rise up on the man's face. "L.A. County Hospital, 1983?" Webb asked.

"I thought you'd remember." The man, short and squat, wore cheap shiny black boots with high heels. He held out his hand, realized that it was caked with grease and dirt, and withdrew it. He turned sideways, so that Webb could see his handiwork. Now crisscrossing jagged red scars heaped up on his forehead, snagging the corner of the upper eyelid, cascading across the man's cheek, ending in a purple swirl just under the angle of his jaw. In addition there were some fresh scratches under one eye, and behind his ear.

"You left a few scars. Think you could fix them up?"

"Sorry, I don't operate any more."

"I saw in the papers. Bet you could use some money, golf clubs, TV set, VCR with stereo and remote. You name it, price is no object."

"Sorry," Webb repeated. He turned to walk away.

The man started after him. "Hey. You some sort of hotshot now?" He laughed, a mean, vicious exclamation. He looked down at Webb's bag, now half-full of rotted bits of garbage. He tugged sharply at it, sending a jolt of pain up Webb's shoulder. "You're just like the others. You may think you're better than the rest of us, but you're not. We're all knee-deep in stink, you included, and don't you forget it."

"I haven't."

"Thanks for nothing."

Webb walked away from the others. He picked at the periphery of the basin, moving along the shadow cast by the freeway. A flock of pigeons swooped down, sniffed at a torn paper bag, and then flew away again. Webb stabbed the bag, and stuffed it inside his sack. He could smell overripe banana.

He approached a rusted corrugated metal drainpipe. He heard scurrying. A large gray rat appeared, a piece of brown apple in its mouth. The rat looked at Webb. Webb did not move. He held his stick poised to strike. The rat drew itself up on its hind legs. It could have been a position of attack or of playfulness. Half a minute passed. Then the rat dropped down and ran back inside the drainpipe.

He'd found his cottage through a local realtor. Compared to his former Santa Monica six-room apartment, it was a dump, but he did not want elegance and order. Faded rugs and a lumpy couch allowed for possibility. Anyone could live there. In his old apartment he would have to be a doctor, attorney, movie director, or drug dealer—someone who could afford two thousand a month. He gave the Venice realtor his polished chrome lamps and plexiglass dining room table in exchange for two months' rent.

A 747 passed overhead. The passengers had destinations. He walked back to his cottage and dropped down onto an easy chair. In a couple hours it would be dark.

He'd jammed the box holding his diplomas and honor society commendations behind the ironing board in the hall closet. So many cancelled tickets, he thought. His medical books went in the storage bin on the back porch. Two other boxes contained his collection of art books. They were mostly Grecian, ranging from early Minoan pottery to several books on Hellenistic vases. Red on black, black on red. He adored the simple lines, the elegance. He had taken drawing courses at UCLA extension. Later he'd enjoyed sketching prospective changes for his patients.

He looked down at his hands. He missed not touching his patients, the easy arm around the shoulder, the pat on the back, the idle hand on an elbow or a knee as he removed sutures or checked a wound. He even missed the small talk, the conversations that normally might annoy and be quickly brushed aside. How long for the sutures to be removed? Why is the scar still red? Will the puckering go away?

He opened one of the books on Greek vase paintings and

slowly traced the delicate features of a young maiden, his hand running back and forth along her face, her outline alive and breathing under his finger. He imagined the pleasure of a vase-maker, who, day after day, turned out beauty as simply as baking bread, unaware that two thousand years later he would be considered a great artist. Webb had felt such moments of satisfaction in his work, but it never seemed enough. Maybe it was the patient's personality— grating, demanding, not sufficiently appreciative—or it could be his own dissatisfaction with an unresolved line of tension causing a wrinkle or a suggestion of a frown. Or his regret that beauty was not an end in itself.

When he awoke it was still dark, the bedroom furniture dense and shadowy. He switched on the metal goose-neck lamp, exposing the few pieces of worn furniture to the harsh light. His muscles ached, his left shoulder was sore, there was a damp spot on his shorts. He rose unsteadily and inspected his face in the bathroom mirror. He slapped some water on his face.

Toast and coffee would make it seem like a normal morning. Except that it was not yet morning. A blackened sky was framed in the bathroom window. Webb turned away from his reflection.

He returned to bed but could not sleep. He checked his nightstand and the kitchen cabinets for a hidden cache of pills, but his cleanup had been thorough. Warm milk, he had once prescribed. Fuck warm milk, I need a drink. He slipped on pants, a shirt and loafers and started out the door, headed for Oblivion, the corner bar. No, he told himself, turning around and sitting on the edge of his bed.

It was easy, just a matter of willpower. He slid out of his clothes and under the covers. Turning back was a minor victory.

At 5:00 A.M., still unable to sleep, he made a cup of instant espresso: two heaping teaspoons. The water boiled slowly in an aluminum saucepan, Webb staring into the gathering agitation. A bubble would form at the bottom, wiggle and shimmy until it freed itself from the tension holding it to the bottom. Then it would rise and pop at the surface. Steam clung to Webb's face as though it were someone else's sweat. He inhaled deeply, sucking the hot wet air into his lungs. He held his breath and felt the steam settling deep within. Once he would have imagined pink buds of alveoli dusted with dew. Dissections corrected that image, taught him that past the age of five minutes a corporate charcoal gray was the norm.

The espresso was hot. The first sip rained acid in his chest. The pain was almost pleasant. To have his organs and muscles suffering their own little agonies seemed appropriate. Soon he would be forty-three; his body was giving notice.

Organs are just bags of cells gathered together and assigned purpose. Early in their development, cells can be anything. Until they are programmed. In the comic opera of his life he had lost his program.

The first week of medical school a classmate stole his skeleton. Find your bones, his professor said. Restoring lost tissues is part of being a doctor.

But someone stole them.

Medicine is competitive. Sink or swim, the prof said.

He took a Tylenol with codeine for the sore shoulder and the rumbling headache working its way up the back of his neck. He considered his alternatives.

Oblivion opened for business at 6:00 A.M. Early hours were a mixture of off-duty cops, taxi drivers, insomniacs, and those who were bracing themselves for the day. Milo Savage, Oblivion's owner, trying to upgrade and attract the local beach-goers walking by, served fresh rolls and fruit juice from six to eight. He held Happy Hour in the evening. All drinks one-third off.

Foot traffic was not all that great at six in the morning. Webb opened the front door. He stopped short. Live music at this hour? He cocked his head and listened as a pianist, invisible behind the upright, knocked out "It Don't Mean a Thing If It Ain't Got That Swing." He imagined some elderly jazzman playing for his breakfast. The phrasing was impeccable, there was no doubt that the pianist had once been somebody. A half dozen men sat at the bar, eating doughnuts and drinking from shot glasses. Several tapped their feet on the rungs of their stools. They chatted quietly.

And then the song began: Billie Holliday's "Strange Fruit." Raspy and slow. Conversation stopped. The voice was chilling, haunting. Webb drew up a chair at the window, out of sight of the pianist. For the moment he forgot that he wanted a drink. And that he missed Elizabeth.

She finished with Gershwin's "There's a Boat Dat's Leavin' for New York."

"Does that earn me a Bloody Mary and a Danish?" the woman said to Milo, who was wiping glasses behind the bar.

"That, young lady, qualifies you for caviar and a permanent slot at the St. Regis. You can play here any time." Milo put down his dishtowel, reached out, and shook the woman's hand. She was angular, underfed. She wore soft,

31

lace-up leprechaun-type boots, jeans, and a full red cotton blouse. There was a small tear in the seam just under her armpit and Webb could see a sliver of white flesh. Her blouse was clean but wrinkled.

"Jessica," she said, biting into a cheese Danish. "Make that drink heavy on the Tabasco."

The sun rose over the beach and jumped into the room.

"Welcome to Oblivion," Webb said. Jessica nodded. She returned to the piano, sipping her Bloody Mary and playing everything from stride to Bach. Only once did she look up, and that was to see if Milo had refilled her drink. Her dark hair hung over her downward-tilted face, nearly touching the keys. Twice men from the bar addressed her, but she did not acknowledge them.

Webb noticed that she had nice breasts. He wondered if she had long tapered toes to match her fingers. He guessed she was in her late twenties. He nursed his whiskey, not even finishing the single shot.

The sun sneaked over the edge of the piano. Jessica slipped on green-rimmed sunglasses, played "Over the Rainbow," rose and asked Milo if she could have a steady job.

"It'll have to be days. The evening pianist's into me for July's wages. Maybe in August, after he's put in his time, we'll see. Meanwhile, it'll have to be breakfast and tips."

"Thanks. And don't worry. I'm not a big eater."

"Need a walk home?" Webb offered.

"Sure, I'm only two blocks away." Which turned out to be the cottage next to Webb's. "It's a friend's," Jessica said, as if explaining how she could afford two rooms and a kitchen.

Webb felt like he was on a date. He shook her hand, said good morning, and left her.

He slept until mid-afternoon, on his couch, in his jeans and socks. He had the feeling that he was about to have a pleasant dream. But he was wrong. In his dream he dissected an Irish setter. As he opened the rib cage, the dog whined and blood jetted out. The bleeding didn't stop; the redness was rising over his ankles, his knees, to his hips. The dog was awake, howling, its legs running under the blue sheets. The blood was to Webb's chest, nearly at his throat. From the other side of the operating table an instructor appeared. Not your day, Dr. Smith?

I guess not, Webb said. There was the taste of blood in his mouth. He awakened and fingered a welt on his tongue. It was bleeding.

He stepped out onto the porch, without any clear intention.

He walked past a series of bungalows and single-story cottages in various states of decay; indoor furniture squatted in front yards of weed, together with dismantled cribs and rusted baby buggies. Front porches sagged on rotten underpinnings. Daytime TV competed with the traffic noise from Canal Street. Venice rents were high; he should be grateful to have found a place only three blocks from the beach.

Webb peered through the faded, half-ripped blinds of the kitchen window, watching. Two muscular young men were delivering Jessica's piano. One man wore a T-shirt rolled up to the shoulders. His muscles rippled as he lifted the front of the upright over the lip of the front porch. The other man did not wear a shirt. He appeared carved from black marble. Small beads of perspiration glistened between his shoulder blades. Webb cringed. These men were Herculean in strength, capable of carrying their own destinies. They were actually smiling as they dragged the piano inside.

Uptown, his colleagues checked operating room schedules, drank coffee in the doctors' lounge, listened to conferences, wondered if they were eating enough fiber. They would phone their brokers, their mechanics, their wives and mistresses—and sense continuity. Even if they hated what they did and told their confidantes that they did daily laps in the quiet despair of routine.

Abruptly he turned around, as though Elizabeth might be watching him. But the room was silent and empty. He had no need for excuses. He could be celibate, a Peeping Tom, or have a different woman every night. It would make no difference. But since Elizabeth's departure he had little desire.

"You bastard," Elizabeth had said when she first found out about the women, throwing a sleek, red Italian telephone at his head. Webb ducked, the phone knocked over a glass end table. There was the sound of shattering glass and then the incessant beeping of the unhooked phone lying among the shards of glass. She threw a vase, a plate, his transistor radio. The barrage over, Elizabeth collapsed on the living room couch, sobbing to the accompaniment of the beeping telephone. Webb put the telephone back on the hook before taking Elizabeth by the shoulders and trying to comfort her.

"They didn't mean anything," he said.

"One day you'll be old. The sun won't revolve around your sex life. You better get plenty good at solitaire so you'll have something to do." She brushed his hand from her shoulder.

The gesture excited Webb. He reached down to stroke her

34

chin. "Come on. It was completely childish. I admit it. Let me apologize." He tried to embrace her.

"You must be kidding." Elizabeth grabbed the incriminating Bel Air Motel matchbook. "Haven't you had enough for one day? You must think I'm stupid." She'd thrown the matchbook at Webb's groin. It fell at his feet. "Thank God we don't have kids."

The memory of Elizabeth's expression of incredible hurt loomed up frequently now, unexpectedly. He wanted to start over again; he needed her forgiveness. But since the separation Elizabeth refused his telephone calls. He'd told Milo, as often as Milo was willing to listen, that he was a perfect bastard. Milo agreed, which accomplished nothing.

Elizabeth, he said aloud, into the darkening apartment. As he spoke he was aware of Jessica, playing "Satin Doll." She was silky smooth.

He pulled up a wooden kitchen chair, turned it backwards, sat down, his arms and chin resting on the slatted back. The chair was against the window sill. A cool ocean breeze floated over his chin and lower face. He could smell fog, saltwater taffy, and suntan oil.

When the music stopped, it was dark and his chin and neck hurt. Time had passed, and for that he was grateful.

His shoulder hurt worse than this morning. He took his left hand and pulled his right arm far overhead. There was a snapping of ligament and it felt as if something had slid into place. The pain subsided. A simple paramedic's trick.

A dull ache remained, a reminder.

3

Joe Walker was a patient on Four East at Good Hope. Two months ago Joe had phoned Webb, his friend the doctor, complaining of a sticking sensation in his abdomen, and a twenty-pound weight loss. "You think it's anything?" The first sentence, the admission that something was wrong, was always the hardest—the hardest to speak and the hardest to hear.

"Don't worry. It's probably just nerves," Webb had said to Joe. But he hadn't believed himself. Joe wasn't a worrier. He fumed, rebelled, walked off jobs, cussed, fought, but he didn't worry, at least not enough to stop eating. "I'm sure it's nothing, but . . . ," Webb had said. Now he hated to think how blasé he must have sounded. He had referred Joe to the head of gastroenterology. The CAT scan revealed an inoperable pancreatic mass.

Joe was trying chemotherapy, but, so far, had experienced all the side effects and none of the benefits. He was wasting away. Webb had gone to see him in the hospital three times in the last week. Joe was thinner and weaker at each visit.

Webb went to pick up a container of won ton soup and an order of chicken with black mushrooms from the take-out restaurant around the corner from the hospital. He stood behind two young nurses buying Chinese dumplings for a staff party. They were in freshly pressed uniforms and smelled of optimism and sense of duty. He had always loved the sight of a nursing uniform tossed alongside his bed. Underwear could be sexy, but the sight of the abandoned shell of a uniform drove him wild. Hospital rules required that all nurses tuck or bun their hair firmly beneath the cap. He loved to undress them, starting at their feet, until they were stark naked, except for their caps. He would slowly unpin the cap, letting their hair fall. He would trace the cap over their bodies, flicking their breasts, running the starched edge between their legs. And then he could be good, good enough for them to tell their friends.

One of the nurses looked up at him and smiled. She seemed so young and innocent. Webb cautiously returned her smile, then picked up his order. The owner motioned toward the nurse, who was now angled away from him, chatting with her friend. He winked at Webb. "Not today," Webb said. "Maybe it's her lucky day."

"Lucky day, yes, lucky day," the owner said. He gave Webb an extra handful of fortune cookies.

Traffic had been terrible; he was hot and sweaty. The back of his shirt was damp and stuck to his skin. Webb slid back into his '76 MG and rounded the corner. He slowed as he drove by the doctors' lot. He recognized several of the cars. He wanted to turn in, knew he shouldn't.

He'd had the same feeling looking at Elizabeth during their settlement conference. He was reminded of Elizabeth's soft skin and the way she gripped the back of his neck when they made love. She often smelled of fresh flowers. She had been wonderful; there had been no reason for others.

The world was treacherous; at any moment he could encounter an OFF LIMITS sign in the most familiar settings.

He parked in the visitors' garage. "Three dollars an hour, to visit the sick? That's highway robbery," he said to the parking attendant.

"Everybody has their price, Dr. Smith," the attendant said.

At the main elevators a clump of doctors stood talking. Their conversation stopped as he approached. Together they rode in silence to the fourth floor. Once he was off the elevator, the other doctors resumed their conversations.

Four East—oncology—was slow. Joe had a private room at semi-private rates.

"Chicken soup. I made it myself," Webb said to Joe. He cleared off the meal tray, sticking the green Jell-O and plastic chicken on the window sill. He ladled out some won ton soup. Joe loved Chinese food.

Joe pulled himself up in bed. Once large and beefy, he now looked lost in ordinary hospital pajamas. He was propped up on three pillows, his hands grabbed the overhead metal trapeze for support.

Webb leaned down and gave his friend a hug. Their cheeks touched. "It'll be all right," Webb whispered, then drew back. "Eat your soup before the won ton congeal." He pulled up a chair, sat alongside Joe, eating the chicken with black mushrooms straight out of the cardboard box. "Tell me when you're ready for the chicken, and we'll switch."

"You told them to leave out the MSG? That shit always gives me a headache."

"No MSG, no added salt, no pepper."

"Then you finish it. I can't stand chicken that bland."

"I got it for you."

"Well, you eat it and see what I've been going through." Joe spooned up the soup slowly, sipping, then waiting. Not at all like the old Joe who attacked his food, who thought that knives and forks slowed you down. The overhead TV broadcast the Dodgers game. The sound was turned off. A runner made a silent dive into second. Then he jumped up and protested to the umpire. Their chests bumped and the player was thrown out of the game.

"I've got twenty that says the Dodgers win their division. Made it with Monte over at the Glass Crutch," Joe said.

"Why waste your money? The Dodgers are lucky they aren't shipped as a unit to some triple-A town. You might as well kiss your money goodbye."

"I only mentioned it so that if they win, you can collect on the bet."

"Can't I just come and make a friendly visit without you making some morbid comment?"

"If you can't talk about death with your doctor, who can you discuss it with?" Joe blew on a spoonful of soup and took another mouthful. At this rate it would take him half an hour to finish.

"I am not your doctor. I am just an old friend who drops by because he likes to see your ugly face. So why don't you use a little manners, a little discretion, and stick with easy chatter."

"'Cause I can talk with you. And you'd better get used to it, because when they're through with me here, you're taking me home with you. It's either that or I join Mary and her new husband."

"Do you ever see her?" Webb asked. He finished the chicken and threw the empty carton in the wastebasket.

"She comes now and then. You know the first thing she does when she visits is open the window. 'Let's get a little fresh air,' she says. Then she gives a few blasts with the air freshener. Like it's for my benefit."

"She always struck me as being a real sizzler. Full of fire."

"She was. But she wanted her fire in a nice two-story ranch house. 'A good fuck is one thing, a matching bedroom set is another.' Her words. The poor woman had aspirations. Maybe if I'd been a plastic surgeon. Not that it did you any good. Man, you really fucked it up."

Joe looked over at Webb. "You had it all, right here." He pointed to the palm of his skinny hand. IV tubing trailed onto the bed. "I could understand if it was me. But you sacrificed all those years. I remember when you'd drag yourself over to my apartment, let's see, I was married to Lynn then. And you fell asleep right in your food. Dead tired. And we admired you, all those hours in the hospital. You must have known you would get caught. Secret wish for self-destruction, that's how I peg it. You have a better explanation?"

"Not that makes sense. At the time it seemed like the right thing to do."

"You got any money left?" Joe asked.

"Not a cent. I had to use my old furniture for the security deposit on my new place. I'm going to have to come up with something pretty soon. But there isn't much market for unlicensed doctors. Maybe I'll drive a cab, sell health insurance. Shit, I don't know."

Webb stared at the floor.

Joe watched the baseball game. Outside the overhead page announced a Code Blue on Ten West. Joe wiped his mouth with a napkin. A piece of won ton hung from his lower lip. Webb was going to mention it but he didn't.

"I've got a small pension from the VA," Joe said. "Not much, but it'll help with the rent."

"Thanks, but I don't need charity."

"It's not charity. I'd be pulling my weight, for my room. Your new place does have an extra bedroom, right?"

"You really don't have anywhere else to go?"

Joe shook his head.

"I'll think of something."

For several minutes the two men remained silent. Webb leaned back in his chair, his head resting against the cool Naugahyde. He was comfortable with Joe. Even their silences were easy. When Joe was gone, he would be without a true friend.

Webb and Joe had been teamed together when Watts broke out—Joe, the driver, Webb, the assistant. They had been sitting on the back steps of the ambulance dispatch garage, smoking a little dope—not enough to impair judgment, Joe insisted—when they got the call.

Webb ran through the smoke, carrying his bag of medical supplies. A young black man was sprawled on the sidewalk in front of a smoldering stereo store, his belly ripped open. Part of his shirt still hung from a shard of glass in the punched-out front window. He'd tripped while trying to lift a TV through the window. The shattered set lay at his feet.

A mass of angry faces watched from doorways and parked cars. Others gathered in the street, armed with rocks. Several of the men carried sticks, some had handguns. Though there was no gunfire, Webb ducked as he ran toward the fallen man. He looked down at the wound, at the blood welling up. The belly button was *missing*. Joe had the man's head resting on a wadded-up blanket. He was trying to start an IV. Webb took some gauze and pulled back the edges of the wound. There was a single arterial spurter. Webb stuck his finger in the wound, pressed firmly. The bleeding stopped.

"I've got it," Webb said to Joe. "You have a hemostat?"

Joe searched through Webb's bag but found nothing. "Fuck. Double, triple fuck. You're supposed to be completely stocked." The two men looked at each other.

"Sorry," Webb said.

"Sure," Joe said.

The injured man was looking at Webb, his eyes large. "You forgot. Perfect. Whitey trash forgot." The man glared. Then his face went momentarily soft as he saw Webb's hand deep within his belly. "Am I going to make it?" he asked in a whisper.

"No sweat," Webb said. "Joe'll drive, and I'll keep this little mother from bleeding. That is, if you don't mind whitey riding in the back with you. Now get a couple of your friends over here to get you into the ambulance."

Joe motioned to the men at the front of the crowd. No one moved. "Don't everyone rush forward at once," Joe said. Someone from the back threw a rock. Webb jerked his head, though the rock was wide of the mark, striking a metal power pole with a *bong*. "Okay, then we'll leave him," Joe said.

Two older men came forward. "That's better," Joe said. The two men started to lift, but they were out of synch. The injured man rolled sideways. Webb lurched forward, his face nearly in the wound. The bleeding started again; Webb remained crouched as he groped in the wetness, poking until he found the nubbin of transected artery. He squeezed again, the artery compressed between his finger and the front of a vertebral body. His hand was nearly hidden from sight; flaps of abdominal wall fell against his wrist. His fingers began to cramp. Webb tried to ignore the ache spreading into his forearm.

"You okay?" Joe asked.

"I think so." The two men lifted again, on the count of three. The crowd moved closer, pressing in as they approached the ambulance. Webb's fingers throbbed; he hoped there wasn't much traffic on the way to L.A. County. He tried not to look at his hand inside the man's abdomen.

Joe had the plasma running; he suspended the bottle from a hook on the ceiling of the ambulance as the two men eased the wounded man inside and onto a gurney. Joe jumped down from the rear of the ambulance. The crowd formed a semicircle, moving in, surrounding him. Webb was seated alongside the gurney watching the crowd grow ugly. A cascade of stones pelted the ambulance. Joe ran to the front and started up the motor. Webb pulled the rear doors closed, one at a time, with his free hand.

"Nice group of friends you've got there," Joe hollered from the driver's seat. "Like the old saying, 'No good deed goes unpunished.'" The rain of stones continued until they rounded a corner.

"I don't make it, you're one dead man," the man said.

"That'll make two of us," Webb said.

He surprised Webb by smiling. The ambulance hit a rough stretch of road, the man wincing with each bump. There was a crown of sweat on his forehead. He put his right hand on Webb's forearm, as though helping to brace it. The two men looked at each other.

"Does it hurt?" Webb asked.

"Only when you jiggle your hand."

"Don't you worry. I'm as steady as stink on shit."

A burst of gunfire rang out in the street. The man twitched with each barrage. The ambulance swerved; Webb's hand slipped. "Christ," he said, feeling his way through blood and intestine.

"I don't think I'm going to make it," the man said.

"You'd better. You don't think I'm doing this for my health, do you?" Webb found the artery and stopped the bleeding, this time with his thumb.

The ride to the hospital, normally no more than ten minutes, took nearly forty, Joe choosing back streets and alleys to avoid cordoned-off areas and regions of maximum fighting. An emergency room doctor clamped the man's severed artery while they were still in the ambulance. The injured man looked up at Webb as he was carried from the ambulance. Webb thought there might have been a trace of gratitude in his eyes. He was not sure.

Moments later the surgical director of the trauma unit emerged and congratulated Webb on his good work. He offered to write Webb a recommendation to medical school.

Webb was back in Watts later that evening.

It was Webb's job on these hospital visits to balance Joe's checkbook and take care of his mail. He sat for a few minutes, sorting his friend's checks: rent, phone, dry cleaning, insurance premiums. The smallness of the desire—to die in balance—alarmed Webb. He put the checks back in their manila envelope. "All done."

"Some guys never make it this far."

"Yeah." Webb took Joe's hand and held it between his. His skin was cool and dry.

"You remember how scared we were when we did Watts?"

Webb nodded.

"Five days of nonstop blood and guts." He sighed and looked off at the ceiling. "That was the life," Joe said. "And afterwards. All those foxy nurses going down on our stories. We were real heroes, weren't we?"

"Something like that," Webb said.

The door opened. Dr. Breslow, the oncologist, poked his head in. "Oh, you have a visitor. I'll come back later."

"Come on in. I've got plenty of time." Webb stood up and faced Breslow. For a moment Breslow just looked at Webb; then he firmly grasped Webb's hand. Breslow's hand was cold and clammy; Webb knew the feeling of dread, making rounds of the dying. He took his hat off to oncologists; they had a special kind of dedication. Webb had worked with Breslow on several post-mastectomy reconstructions. He appreciated Breslow's thoroughness and his gentle manner. He had specifically asked for him to manage Joe's case.

Webb patted Breslow on the shoulder. "Good to see you." Breslow pulled back Joe's covers. He poked gingerly, feeling Joe's belly, then his legs. He listened to his chest, bracing Joe with his other hand. Joe watched Breslow's face, interpreting. "Any new pains?" Breslow asked.

Joe shook his head.

Breslow straightened up and pulled his white lab coat tight around him. "Any plans?" he asked Webb in the same tone he had used to Joe.

Webb shook his head.

"Personally, I think you got the shaft. I'm really sorry." Breslow closed the door quietly behind him.

Webb walked over to the bed and gave Joe a final hug. He could feel his friend's frail hand, trailing its IV, grasp his shoulder. Webb grabbed him by both ears. "You stay out of trouble, you hear me?" he said.

He slowed as he passed the nursing station. They were making chart rounds. He dipped his hand into the medicine cart and took a handful of vials. His pockets rattled with plastic hope as he inched back home to Venice.

Again he awoke too early. He let an hour pass before going out for breakfast.

"Why the wet eyes yesterday?" Jessica asked.

" 'Strange Fruit.' It always chokes me up." Webb sipped his orange juice. The sun was not yet up; the beach was a strip of fuzzy grayness at the base of Oblivion's front window. The underside of the clouds closest to the horizon had the barest traces of pink.

"Did you ever see Billie Holiday?"

"I'm not that old. I've seen documentaries, that's all."

"Those were the days," Jessica said. She doodled at the piano. No specific tune, just a progression of chords and, occasionally, a few bars of melody that she sandwiched in between sips of her Bloody Marys. Milo stood behind the bar, his hands playing with the keys of the old National Cash Register. An orange NO SALE sat in the register window.

"She was beautiful," Jessica said. "Pain and suffering tattooed into her face. In the pictures. You look at her, you know what it's like to be a real woman."

"I saw her," Milo said. "At Birdland. Billie and Lester Young. You could have heard a pin drop."

"What year?" Jessica asked.

"Early fifties. I can't remember."

"And you've seen Coleman Hawkins, Thelonious Monk. And Charlie Parker, you've heard him?"

Milo smiled and nodded.

"I am one jealous woman," Jessica said. She put down her drink and launched into an upbeat rendition of "Straight, No Chaser."

At the conclusion of the song, Jessica said, "They were friends, Thelonious and Billie. They jammed together at Monk's place. I read that somewhere." Jessica brushed back her hair, then massaged the base of her neck, at the same time looking under the piano, as if searching for a lost tune. Webb began to speak, but Jessica put her finger to her lips, and gave a slight shake of her head.

He was reminded of a startled deer facing oncoming headlights. A deer with a troubled past. He went to the counter, picked out an almond croissant and a banana, and placed the plate on the piano next to her Bloody Mary.

Jessica reached out with her left hand, took the croissant and began nibbling, without looking at her food or at Webb. She continued to stare at the foot pedals. She hummed softly, as though she were about to speak. She bobbed to an unheard rhythm. Then, with a single finger, she began picking out a melody. Single notes, a few bars, silence, a note or two. She put her arm on the music stand of the piano, her head rested in the crook of her arm. She stayed this way for some time.

Milo looked at Webb and shrugged. Webb had been dropping by Oblivion since he moved to Venice, and the two men had developed an affection for each other. Milo was New York: streetwise, gruff, and warm. Webb liked his raw edges. Before his wife died and he moved to California, Milo had owned a bar on Broadway near Fifty-fourth Street. Now the side walls of his bar were filled with pictures: Casey Stengel, Manolete, Mayor LaGuardia, Picasso holding his grandchild, and an aerial view of Times Square on New Year's Eve. A red paper arrow pointed to a small black dot in the center of the picture. "That's me," Milo would often say, as though getting his bearings. The two men looked at each other, and at Jessica, and drew her into their circle of friendship.

"Bad day," Jessica said, finally. "Melody must be on strike." She pulled the piano cover over the keys. "It's sometimes like that."

"Hey, no big deal. There's just us early birds and the insomniacs," Milo said.

"No. I mean either they're not broadcasting, or I'm not receiving." She looked at the two men, and then suddenly broke into a marvelous, low-pitched belly laugh. "You guys look at me like I'm crazy. No such thing. I merely meant that these aren't my tunes. They're their tunes, floating around, waiting to be properly played. Some days you hear them, some days you don't." She rubbed her fingers, wiped her mouth with her sleeve, and downed her drink in a single gulp. She stepped back from the piano, pirouetted and made a deep bow. "We are sorry for any interruption in your service. Power will be restored as soon as the source of the failure can be found." She flipped off the fake Tiffany lamp over the piano.

"Want to hear the ocean?" Webb asked.

Jessica slipped her arm in Webb's; the touch of her hand on his forearm reminded him of how long it had been. They stepped out into the gathering brightness.

It was a Wednesday morning. Stores were closed; the beach was nearly empty, except for those jogging through the sand. The usual assortment of musicians, jugglers, skaters, and sidewalk hustlers had not arrived. Yet the weight lifting pavilion was jampacked. He and Jessica strolled up the pathway at a distance, watching. A gargantuan black weight lifter struggled beneath a massive barbell. A sparse group of spectators—mostly heavily-muscled fellow lifters—urged him on. He was going for the beach record, someone said.

The black man had the weight against his chest, his knees wobbly beneath him. He pushed; the weight rose unsteadily overhead. One of the other lifters kept insisting that he had to straighten his elbows completely. The black man flashed him a look of anger and pushed harder. He froze, the weight wavering, his body and arms no longer rising, not yet falling, a quivering monument to defeat. Then the weight fell forward, landing in the soft dirt at his feet. The lifter followed, collapsing alongside his barbell.

The crowd watched, waiting for the man to rise. Two men nearest to him bent down. The black man remained lifeless in the dirt. One ran for the phone, another checked for a pulse. Webb started forward, pushing through the spectators, but by the time he reached the man, CPR was already in progress. They were doing a perfectly adequate job. The fallen man was stirring; he opened his eyes.

"Did I make it?" he asked.

"Yeah, you made it," one relieved lifter said. He held the black man's head on his knee, dabbed at his forehead with a sleeve of a sweat shirt. "You set the beach record," he said quietly. The black man smiled weakly and gave a thumbs-up sign as two ambulance attendants eased him onto a stretcher. The crowd began to disperse.

I am a doctor, Webb was going to say, but there had been no need. And to be accurate, he would have had to say, I am a suspended doctor.

He rejoined Jessica. They continued down the beach, taking off their shoes and walking in the sand, heading towards the surf.

"Milo says you're very good."

"How would he know?" Webb said.

"He says he can tell. He told me the whole story."

"Are you humoring me?" Webb stopped and held Jessica by the shoulder. A surfer disappeared under the crest of a wave, then reappeared, one hand raised in a victory salute.

"Probably. I'm a sucker for a good-looker with a first-rate sob story, so I tell myself you had decent reasons, that you cared. If I'm wrong, no big deal. I've made plenty of mistakes before. But a word of warning. If you're going to be a calloused insensitive son of a bitch, and you know it, why not tell me in advance and save us both the trouble."

"I'm a calloused indifferent son of a bitch," Webb said. He brushed a strand of hair from Jessica's cheek.

Jessica stared into Webb's eyes. "I wish I weren't such a shitty judge of character," she said, taking Webb's hand.

"But when you don't know yourself, how are you supposed to be able to read the other guys?"

A bearded man in filthy cutoffs and combat boots walked by, carrying a bedroll over his shoulder. "Don't feel like the Lone Ranger. Around here self-doubt is the common denominator," Webb said. "I could have insisted the kid go to County. The more I think about it, the more I have to believe that it was just a case of my arrested development. Always trying to prove something."

"Most charity works that way. But sandwiched in between all the bullshit acts is the occasional real thing. Maybe you really wanted to help. That's more than most people are capable of."

"Sounds pretty feeble."

"Please. We started out to have a romantic walk."

It was a cloudless day; sea gulls soared on invisible warm air currents. The beach was beginning to fill with intrepid sunbathers and kids with their dogs. A boy ran by pulling a large kite in the shape of a dragon. The dragon stared down at Webb with its fixed expression. The boy was all smiles.

The two walked in the surf, Webb holding both of their shoes in his free hand. His loafers were stiff and clunky in comparison with her flats, which were as light as two flowers.

Elizabeth adored the ocean. Elizabeth: a sales rep from a company that made silastic prostheses and inserts. They had met over a convention hall display of artificial chins, cheekbones, and breast implants. Elizabeth had her own promotional book of befores and afters, demonstrations of children with reshaped faces. She had gathered the pictures from satisfied clients: surgeons who now endorsed her products.

Webb loved the look in her eye as she proudly demonstrated someone else's work. Elizabeth slowly made her way through the photo album as if she were showing off her own children.

Elizabeth had wanted to go to medical school but had feared biochemistry and physics. She'd majored in business, took only the simplest of science classes, and developed an exaggerated sense of admiration for anyone smart enough to complete the courses she had ducked. Knowing that Webb had started with nothing, that he had waited tables and dug ditches during high school, been an ambulance paramedic to work his way through college, then borrowed his tuition to medical school, sealed their romance. He could do no wrong.

Near the end, they'd walked along the surf and wondered what had happened.

"Talking to you is hopeless," she'd said. "You have all the answers. And none of them make any sense. The doctors at the hospital are quacks, the professors at the university want a rat in every bed, plastic surgery is nothing more than being a glorified beautician. Every day it's the same litany of complaints. And then you use the failures of others to explain your drinking and chippying around. What a waste."

She stepped back from the surf, turned and started toward the car. Webb started after her.

"Come on. Give me another chance." He caught up with her, but she spun away.

"Too much damage," Elizabeth said, waving him away.

Too much damage, Webb heard above the waves.

Criticize and retreat had become the main movements in his life, the dance steps of avoidance.

Jessica bent down and threw some water on her face, her cheeks glistening in the morning light. She tossed back her head, her dark hair sweeping across her shoulders. She was lovely, and she was now looking at him as though she knew what he was thinking and it made her happy.

They headed for the lighthouse. Jessica hummed occasionally. He reached behind Jessica and put his arm around her shoulders. They walked that way for some distance, then Jessica unfurled herself, skipping away, doing a cartwheel in the sand. Running up the beach, she stopped long enough to watch him watching her. She waved, and ran on. Webb remained motionless, the surf washing up around his feet, creating two sandy parentheses. He would have to hang on for dear life, he thought, as he started up the beach after her, first walking, then breaking into a run.

He had loved Elizabeth; he still loved her. He ran faster, the salt air stinging his face. He ran harder, the sea air tight in his chest. He struggled for breath, slowed, and slid down in the sand. Jessica ran up the dozen steps to the lighthouse and beckoned. Webb pointed to his chest and wiped his brow. She crooked her finger and licked her lips. And Webb was up again, running toward the lighthouse, his steps thick in the wet sand, his legs heavy and stiff, his heart pounding.

4

Webb sat at the bar and looked through the employment section of the L.A. *Times*. Except for the most menial jobs, he was completely unqualified. He paused at Ambulance Drivers. They all required emergency medical technician licenses. His had expired during his residency. There had been no reason for renewal. He doubted that he could be recertified. Webb knew enough about state laws to realize that being a suspended doctor wouldn't help.

Milo gave him coffee.

Webb continued scouring the ads. Nothing struck him as reasonable. He sat for some time, deliberating. Down the street a new medical clinic was in its final stages of construction. They would need triage doctors. Normally they would be hiring guys fresh out of internship—little experience meant low pay.

"You think that new clinic would hire me, even without a license?" He looked at Milo.

"You're hot shit on paper. They'd probably sign you on the spot. Chances are ten-to-one that they won't ask to actually see your license. You scrub your face, get the hairs under your chin that you've missed for the last few weeks, slip into some fresh clothes, and you go on over there. I'd say you're a cinch."

"Plastic surgeon one day, sore throat and hangnail specialist the next. What a comedown. Or, maybe it's the other way around."

"You have a better idea for rent money?"

"You know, you'd have made a real nice wife." Webb reached out and playfully patted Milo on the cheek. "Always there when I need you, always looking out for my best interest. If only you weren't so ugly."

"Maybe you could fix me up just the way you want me. Everyone says you were the best."

"Who's everyone?"

"Well, Red, for one. Right, Red?" Milo called to a sunburned bar regular, his Hawaiian sport shirt soiled and torn. His deeply calloused heels hung over the crushed backs of his tennis shoes. He sat at the end of the bar nursing a double shot of vodka with a decaf coffee back. A small pile of wet sand drifted up between his feet.

"Absolutely," Red said. "The very best. Everyone says so. Even Al and Pete here." Red elbowed his two wasted drinking buddies. They looked up from their respective reveries and nodded. "Everyone at this end's in agreement." He lifted his shot glass in a salute.

Webb raised his coffee cup, returning the salutation. He turned to Milo. "I think I'll take a shot at the clinic."

"Tell them you're a Vietnam vet and you'll torch the place if they don't hire you." Milo leaned against the back counter and wiped his hands on his pants. "And do me a favor, cut out the maudlin shit. It's bad for business." Milo indicated the empty bar stools to either side of Webb.

INSTANTCARE
OPEN TWENTY-FOUR HOURS
ALL INSURANCE ACCEPTED

The sign—a soft purple neon on a champagne background—hung over the converted store. The waiting room could be seen behind drawn beige Levelor shades. Up on a ladder, the sign-maker was easing a pink neon face, smiling and bespectacled, into the space just beyond Insurance Accepted.

"Who's that?" Webb called. He was standing on the sidewalk in front of the building. The store next door sold Day-Glo paintings and sports car posters, with long-legged women draped over Alfa hoods.

"That's your new family doctor," the sign man said. "I bent him myself."

"Bent?"

"Blew him from glass. Bent the tubing. Whipped him into shape. It's too bad I couldn't do the same with my own doctor." The sign man got on and off his ladder, repeatedly checking to be certain the doctor's chin was even with Insurance Accepted. He cocked his head, looked at the face from different angles. "It's not quite what I had in mind," he said, finally. "In the shop he looked more dignified. Maybe it's the pink, but maybe it's the chin. What do you think?"

"It's the chin all right. It should be stronger."

"I don't know. I kind of like the softness. It tells me the doctor is listening."

"No. You listen with the eyes. Put a little blue in the iris."

"There aren't any eyes, just glasses."

"That's what I mean. Deep blue eyes rimmed in purple. I would imagine that would be very impressive."

"Sometimes I'm sorry I ever moved to California," the sign man said. He folded up his ladder and slid it onto the roof of his truck. He made a final assessment of the neon, shrugged, and stepped into his truck. He closed the door gently, lingered a second, then pulled away from the curb.

"**Y**ou have any references?" Angel Williams said. He was a short, fat, bald man, with greasy skin and a faint glimmer of perspiration on his upper lip. The lower lip retreated into a vestigial chin. He wore white shoes and a seersucker suit. Behind his desk was a smaller version of the neon Instantcare sign out front. His head was backlit in purple, the dome of his head glowing as though radioactive.

"I'll bring in my diplomas, if you like."

"Yeah, that's good." Mr. Williams studied Webb's résumé. "You used to do faces. Why would you stoop to work for wages?" He tapped his pencil on Webb's résumé.

"I wanted to get back into real medicine."

"Sure. Hold out your hands." Webb was grateful for the Valium. Williams pulled up Webb's left sleeve to the elbow, inspected his forearm. "One look is worth a thousand denials." Williams squinted, gave Webb the once-over. "No, you look okay, just a little run of bad luck, huh? Gambling, women, the market, you don't have to say. It doesn't matter, it's all the same to me."

Williams consulted a schedule on his far wall. "Right now, all we have is graveyard. Frankly, if I were a doctor, I'd prefer the small hours. Less sniffles, more real stuff, except for the bad dreams. I presume you've had enough psych to handle the weirdos."

Webb nodded.

"Good."

Williams had diplomas: BA in economics, MBA, a degree in hospital administration. He saw Webb reading his credentials. "I used to be in hospitals, but that's not where the action is any more. This is my sixth shop. Question: How many operations does it take to make a chain? You know what the answer is? One more. Always one more. You do a good job and maybe I'll give you some warrants, options, rights. You look like a man who could do with some options. Okay? You start tomorrow. Oh," he said, rising from his swivel chair and advancing his hand, "you can call me Angel."

He did not ask for Webb's license.

"I'm not terminal enough," Joe said to Webb. He smiled feebly, pulled himself up in bed, and took a sip of water. His torso was covered with food crumbs: bits of bread, banana, and smudges of yellow Jell-O. A single stalk of asparagus lay beneath two ridges of bunched-up sheet like a dozing slug. "Sorry about the mess," he said, brushing some of the food onto the floor. His hair was matted in back, there was a pillow crease carved into his cheek. "I guess I dozed off."

His hand trembled as he held the paper cup to his mouth. Webb looked away and hoped Joe wouldn't notice. He did.

"Some smiling nurse from Utilization Review tells me that I should plan on leaving—insurance doesn't cover nonacute care. Tells me they've got me lined up at a hospice. Like she's doing me some great favor. I've checked. The one she's so kindly signed me up with has mostly AIDS patients. I'll get to sit in some crappy rented living room, an afghan over my feet, and listen to old Carmen Miranda records."

The upper third of his abdominal incision rose between the flaps of his pajama top like a deep red exclamation point. Joe buttoned up, the wound that exposed his disease now tucked behind his personal blue cotton curtains. The buttoning added another fifteen years to Joe's apparent age. Old men buttoned all the way to the throat. Joe was one stop away.

"What are the choices?" Webb asked.

"You remember the night at the Glass Crutch when you picked up that honey? What were you then, a freshman in med school? Thought you knew it all. You're all over her, telling her that she was at a personal crossroad, that she could either come with you or spend the rest of her life with her bozo truckdriver husband drinking Seven and Sevens. And you've got your hand halfway down her blouse, when her husband comes back from the head. How big was he, come on, you tell me."

"Six-five, minimum."

"Weight?"

"Two-fifty, how should I know? It was dark."

"Not that dark that he couldn't see you drooling on his lovebird. And the tire iron in his hand?"

Webb nodded.

"And what happened next? You remember?"

"Yeah, you screamed *'Fire,'* he turned, you belted him in the mouth, and we were out the back door." Webb laughed as he spoke.

"And then what did you say? Back in my car, the windows rolled up, the doors locked, us cruising out into traffic."

" 'I could have taken him. One solid punch. No big deal.' "

"I knew you'd remember. Come on, tell me what else you said, just in case I got it wrong."

"Something about I owed you one."

"So it's collection time. And that's just in case you want a concrete example. Which you don't need, because we're buddies, right?" Joe coughed, at the same time holding his lower rib cage. He wiped his mouth with small tissue which he dropped in a white paper bag taped to his nightstand. The bag was nearly full.

Webb walked to the window, stared out at the procession of doctors' cars streaming in and out of the lot. It was late morning; the departing cars would be taking their drivers back to their offices. The arriving cars were dropping off those lunching at the hospital. It was very neat and tidy, the movements as predictable as tides, week after month after year, the asphalt surface of the lot wearing out, getting repaved, the doctors getting older, getting bypasses and endarterectomies and holes drilled in their prostates. The inevitability of routine made Webb's skin crawl; now his friend was asking to come to live with him, Webb responsible for emptying the little bags for his tissues, for changing his sheets, ultimately even wiping his ass.

"Please, Webb. I promise I won't take long."

Webb turned, now facing Joe. They had been a team, the two of them in the County ambulance, passing the hours like chatty long-lost brothers. Webb had worked with Joe for a while after college, until he had saved enough for med school. Joe stayed on, briefly, then fell into a variety of other jobs. They remained close. Whenever Webb wanted to talk, it was Joe he phoned. And when there was nothing to say, when he just wanted to get out, it was the two of them that went drinking, to the track—Santa Anita, Hollywood Park, wherever Joe had the hottest tip—to the Dodgers' games, boxing at the Forum. Or they would grab a quick sandwich, tell a few jokes, just to check in with each other.

They knew as much about each other as the other was willing to reveal.

"You take the smaller bedroom, and you keep the window open," Webb said.

"Anything you say, boss."

Angel Williams sat behind his highly lacquered desk. Webb stood in front, flanked by four other doctors and several nurses and technicians. It reminded Webb of his first day of internship or residency, his first day anywhere working for the other guy. Time for the company philosophy, the indoctrination speech. Then you get out in the front lines and duck the bullets.

Behind his high-backed swivel chair, propped against a matching leather wastepaper basket, was a detailed architectural model of the clinic. From his position Webb had an aerial view of the entire first-floor layout; it was immediately apparent that Angel Williams's office was bigger than any two examining rooms and was the only room with plants. A scaled-down version of the Instantcare sign, painted in Day-Glo luminescent purple paint, was glued behind Williams's miniature desk. The sign behind Williams's actual desk bathed the back of Williams's head and the mock-up in the same purple glow. Both appeared made of the same material.

"Your job is to practice medicine. Mine is to tell you how." Williams looked down the row of physicians. "You guys know diseases; I know people. Our job is to give patients what they want, keep 'em happy. Good medicine means good word of mouth. Remember, the clinic's not busy, you guys can look elsewhere. According to economic indicators, there are too many doctors; Easy Street is over. So take a listen."

He pointed to the doctor to Webb's left. "Remington. A patient comes in with a sore back. What does he want?"

"Diagnosis and treatment. X-rays, a good exam, a decent explanation of what's wrong, maybe some pain medication for a week or two. It all depends." The young doctor spoke with confidence. He was not prepared for Williams.

"Good textbook answer, but not the Instantcare way. Maybe he wants nothing but a week off work, an excuse not to sleep with his wife, help with the kids. Maybe he is lonely and wants someone to touch him, rub his back. Maybe he's afraid of cancer and wants a written guarantee that it isn't. You got the point? You find out what he wants and give it to him. Determine if it's just pain, or if the guy is suffering."

Remington paused, as though to say something, but changed his mind.

"What's the matter? Does it frost you to have some slob layman tell you how to practice? Well, get used to it. You guys have had it fat for years. Now it's the era of consumerism. We tell you what we want and you deliver the goods. Just keep in mind, you are a technician, a repairman for the body. If it makes you feel better to think you are a healer, fine. If thinking you are a minor god helps you to get to sleep at night, it's okay with me. But keep that arrogant healer bullshit out of the clinic. Keep it simple, down to earth. If you disagree, if you think you are something special, just see how fast your patients leave you if they get a cheaper insurance plan, or free parking elsewhere. So maybe this guy with the backache wants his back rubbed. Fine. Give him a month of physiotherapy. He wants a letter to his boss, fine—but he has to come three times a week for documentation. He wants pills, fine—small amounts, keep him coming, no chance he will sell them.

"Push the clinic. Make the patients want to come back, obliged to come back. Unless, of course, they have prepaid plans; I will be contracting with some as we go along. Then less is better. You all know that there's really no decent treatment for back pain other than exercise. So, if they're prepaid—their charts will be marked with a red star—give them an exercise pamphlet," Williams reached down and pulled a small booklet from his desk drawer, "and tell them God helps he who helps himself.

"But for the most part, our clients will be drop-ins. Fee for service. And we shall respect their wishes. Which means you got to service them, kiss their shiny full-payment asses. Look at chiropractors. They don't know shit and the patients love them. Ask the man on the street who he trusts. Not the prim bow-tied family doc who sits behind his desk with all his diplomas on the wall and looks over his bifocals at his patients. No, they rave about some high school graduate quack, who x-rays their spine and tells them their heart is out of alignment. Why? Because the chiropractors touch, lay on the hands. They're all over their patients, manipulating. What a great choice of words as the slogan for an entire profession. Manipulation. Don't laugh. Take a lesson. When

63

you read patients their prescriptions, step around the desk, put one hand in the small of their back or on their shoulder, look them in the eye, man, look them in the eye, and make the sale. Every patient gets touched, you got that? If I hear that any of you are desk-sitters, you can forget Instantcare.

"Ask about their families. Look interested. Write down their wife's name and at the end of the exam, say something like 'Your wife, Sue, will be happy to know that everything's turned out okay.' Pretty soon, Sue will be a clinic patient, too." Williams stopped, pulled out a handkerchief, and wiped his upper lip and brow.

Webb watched, mesmerized. The hustler had it right on the money. As disgusted as he should have been by Williams's sales pitch, he couldn't help but agree—if the goal was pushing medicine in an area already vastly overpopulated with healers of one sort or another. Not like so many underdeveloped regions of the world where the kids ate tubercle bacillus for dinner, swam in malaria pools, and slept in garbage. Without a doctor in sight. He had considered going abroad and working in one of the volunteer-staffed hospitals. Some of the others from the hospital had gone on two-and-three-month tours—the same doctors who worried about extracting the last dollar from their patients' insurance policies. And they returned to give slide shows at grand rounds, showing photo after photo of the grateful Third World poor they had treated. Webb had watched, annoyed at their smugness, more annoyed that he had not gone. Other staff physicians and nurses were moved and volunteered. The planes left for Vietnam, Central America, Ethiopia, India, and a hundred other destinations, while he touched up noses and augmented tits.

"And if you think the Instantcare approach is crass, you'd

better take another look." Williams held up a handful of brochures. "Scripp's, Mayo, City of Hope, Cedars-Sinai, they're all advertising." He fanned the air with the leaflets before putting them down and picking up an issue of *Gentlemen's Quarterly*. He opened to the middle of the magazine. "This is a list of the leading medical specialists in the country, subdivided by state. Look at the names: almost all university professors. Do you really think they're the best?" Williams read the names of some of the doctors from the Los Angeles area. "You," Williams said, pointing to Webb. "You've been around a few years. You ever hear of these guys?"

"Just for doing research. At UCLA and USC, I think."

"Correct. Absolutely. Half of these guys don't even have a practice. Then how did they get listed? I'll tell you. Because the universities have the most money, the best marketing divisions. I should know. When I was administrator over at Doctor's Hospital—a mere three hundred beds out in the valley—we had a full-time publicist. She knew all the local journalists and TV newspeople. She had to place so many spots per week, or she got canned. But we were peanuts compared to UCLA and USC. They've got real juice, so we read about their marvelous doctors—guys who treat rats and guinea pigs—in *Gentlemen's Quarterly*.

"This guy, Dr. Dan, the one on TV. Right after his internship he studied at Pasadena Playhouse. Not one single day treating patients on his own. He had one of the leading industrial video companies make him a demo tape and his agent sent them to all the stations in the area. Now he's in millions of homes, every day, making his noontime television house calls in that phony, syrupy, low-keyed voice, wiping out thousands of office visits. The women love him.

"Medicine is word-of-mouth. It means TV, radio, newspapers, celebrity endorsements, none of which grows on trees. That's where you doctors come in. The bottom line, gentlemen. If the clinic doesn't make it—that means increasing profits, a minimum of 12 to 15 percent per annum—then you don't make it. Our destinies are intertwined." He meshed his fat little fingers, moving them together and apart.

"All doctors are to dress the same. Khaki chinos, light pink short-sleeved shirts, and medium gray wool ties. This way there is a sense of continuity, even if the individual doctors change. All beards are to be trimmed and nails must be short and clean. I'll be checking." Williams wiped his face with his now-spotted blue silk handkerchief. The indoctrination lecture was over.

The clinic was a former dress shop, newly repainted and decorated. Long and narrow, it was divided by partitions into a series of examining rooms, Williams' office, a central registration-reception area, and a waiting room in front. The colors were subdued beiges and earth tones, and reminded Webb of nouvelle California restaurant decor. Upstairs were the laboratory and two rooms used as sleeping quarters for the night staff. On the day shift the clinic had three physicians, a receptionist, and several nurses and nurse's aides. At night, there was only a single physician, Webb, and a lab tech—Ray Malone—who doubled as a nurse's aide. On opening night the two men sat behind the reception counter, drinking coffee and getting acquainted.

"I'm just temporary," Ray said. "Until the Apocalypse." He pointed to the side counter and the computer used for billing and processing lab data. "I brought my program and the data base from home and slipped it into the machine. Twenty floppy disks of research rolled up into a single daily number. PD, I call it. Probability of Destruction. It's very sophisticated. You give every possible event a numerical coefficient, do a Fourier transform analysis, and bingo. Here, let me show you."

Ray pointed to the screen. Listed alphabetically were major government leaders. Each was assigned a number. Hussein and Gorbachev were .00003, Ghadafy: .0012, Bush: .025. Ray ran through the major political leaders, scrolled down to Chernobyl and Three Mile Island. "These are more difficult. Because of conflicting data the standard deviation is too large. You know anything about probability theory?" Ray asked as a series of equations appeared.

Webb started to answer, but stopped, realizing that Ray was absorbed in typing in numbers, calculating.

"The research librarian over at Santa Monica Public says that the true Chernobyl figures are double those released by the Department of Defense. The Bulletin of Atomic Scientists says triple." He ran some more numbers. "It makes a quarter percent difference in the final figure." He turned to Webb. "Say, did you answer my question?"

"What question?"

"About probability theory. Do you know anything more than what they must have taught you in med school?"

Webb shook his head.

"Shit. Do I have to explain this all to you, or can you take my word?"

"I think your word will do."

The machine whirred away. Ray leaned back, his feet up on the reception counter. He was tall, perhaps six-six, and had scraggly red hair and a freckled face. His eyes were wild. His teeth leaned precariously against each other; one incisor was missing, there were several other dark spaces scattered throughout his mouth. Webb immediately liked him.

"You may not be good for me," Webb said, "but at least you'll be entertaining."

"This is not entertainment. This is reality. The numbers, that is. Okay, so they're symbolic, but they're accurate. Better than anxiety and fear and trembling, more down-to-earth and exact. Why worry about the bomb in the abstract? Give its probability a number, like the chance of rain. Then you can deal with it." Ray had a small involuntary tic at the corner of his eye. He tilted his head so that Webb would not see. The machine stopped and a number appeared above the cursor.

"Point sixteen. That's not bad, considering. I guess I can put away my worries for today."

"Sorry, but they're just beginning." Through the window they could see a young man bent over on the sidewalk, vomiting. His friends stood at a respectful distance and laughed. Beyond was the darkness of the unlit beach and ocean.

"I can't stand the smell of puke," Ray said.

"Then what are you doing as a nurse's aide?"

Ray shrugged as he opened the door and helped the kid into the reception area. He reeked of beer; vomit drenched the front of his T-shirt.

"Got something for the heaves?" the kid asked.

"I'm supposed to ask if you have insurance, but I'll bet you don't." Ray eased the boy into a straight-backed chair near the entrance to one of the examining rooms. The boy gagged, then shook his head.

"I thought this was a free clinic," the kid said. He hiccupped several times and gagged into an already-soaked handkerchief. Webb brought over a blue plastic emesis basin. "Compliments of the house," Webb said. "Next time you drink, be sure to carry insurance. Bend over." The teenager stepped into the examining room and dropped his pants. Webb gave him a shot of Tigan. "Try coating your stomach with milk first. Sometimes that works."

"Thanks," the kid said. He staggered back onto the sidewalk where he was joined by his laughing friends.

"You have a nice touch. You should have been a surgeon. The way you just slipped that needle in. Beautiful."

"Cut the crap. For your information, I am a board-certified plastic surgeon." Ray knew probability theory. He, Webb, knew medicine. He wanted to tell Ray about his good work, about the cleft palate clinic at Shriner's Hospital that he ran for the first three years following his residency, about the 80 percent burn cases that he successfully grafted, and the torn off fingers that he restored to working order. But there was no point. He was now a physician of the dry heaves trying to fill Angel Williams's quota for the night.

"No shit. And you're working here?" Ray stared at Webb. He drummed his fingers on the frame of the keyboard terminal. "And I'm not supposed to ask why, right?"

"Work on the end of the world and be quiet."

Joe was sitting in his wheelchair. Webb took Joe's radio, portable TV, aftershave lotion, a few paperback books, and toilet bag, and stacked them in Joe's lap. It would save Webb an extra trip to the car.

Joe winced and looked down at the sum of his possessions. A nurse handed Webb a plastic bag full of medicines. Webb balanced them atop the TV.

"You think that'll be enough?" Webb asked.

"There's at least a month's worth," the nurse said. She turned her head slightly away from Joe, as if speaking at an angle would prevent Joe from hearing. "If you need more, you can always get them from the oncology service."

Joe saw Webb eyeing the vials. "Those are for me," he said as soon as the nurse left the room.

In the parking lot Webb helped Joe from the wheelchair. He was nearly dead weight. Webb supported him with one arm under his armpit, and one leg braced behind his knee, easing him into the MG. He tried to fit the wheelchair into the small space behind the front seats, but there was only enough room for the radio and TV. He put the chair in the trunk and secured the lid with an old tie he found behind the spare tire in the wheelwell.

"How I love the excitement of moving day," Joe said. He looked straight ahead as Webb maneuvered out of the parking lot. "The glorious freedom of the open road, all your possessions on your back or jammed into your car. The sky's the limit." Joe did not smile. He held a bouquet of flowers his ex-wife had sent him when she heard that Joe was going to move in with Webb. A panel truck abruptly, without a signal, pulled out from the curb, directly in front of the MG. Webb jammed on the brakes and Joe went forward into the dashboard. He braced himself with one hand. The flowers scattered on the floor.

"Hey, asshole, watch where you're going," Webb shouted at the driver, who turned and gave Webb the finger. "Come here and say that," Webb hollered, half-opening his driver's door. The truck driver got out of his truck and walked a few steps towards Webb. He was huge. His battered face reflected a lifetime of fighting. Webb closed his door, backed up, and drove around the driver, gunning his motor as he passed.

"There are more important things in life than being in the right," Joe said.

"You okay?"

"The picture of health."

Joe leaned over, picked up his flowers and stuffed them back into the opaque plastic water container. At the first stop sign, Webb reached down and pulled one last daisy from behind the curled-up floor mat. He slid the single flower into the vase.

Getting Joe out of the car was even more difficult than getting him in. The low seat was difficult for Joe to navigate. His thighs lacked power. Webb tugged and pulled, trying to ease Joe into the wheelchair. Only when he was erect was his strength great enough to enable him to step onto the curb and into the chair. "I don't think I can make it up the stairs," he said quietly, indicating the three wooden steps leading from the sidewalk to Webb's house. Webb tried pushing him up the stairs, then resorted to pulling him up, backwards. By the time he was in the house, Webb's arms were shaky from effort. He recalled the black weight lifter collapsing at the beach.

"Do you remember your CPR?" Webb said to Joe.

"Sure. You don't have a thing to worry about. Now get me into bed, I'm exhausted from the trip."

"Me too."

Webb's cottage had two bedrooms. The back room looked out on a small untended garden of cactus and dusty rose-bushes. It had a western exposure and was filled with noon sunlight. The front room was considerably smaller and dimly lit. Its single window faced a narrow concrete walk-way and a row of aluminum garbage cans. Webb stood in the hallway silently debating. The bathroom opened directly into the back room. The front room was on the other side of the kitchen. Webb imagined the terminal stages, Joe in front. He would have to carry Joe's bedpan down the hall, past the kitchen. It would stink up the house.

He slipped into the back room, changed the sheets, took

out his few belongings, came back into the hallway, and rolled Joe into his new quarters.

Joe turned to Webb. "Don't worry. I won't take long. Then you can have your old room back."

"No hurry. The darker room will make it easier for me to sleep in the daytime."

As Webb positioned Joe in bed, the fog rolled in and doused the sunlight. Joe watched the sun dip beneath the grayness, then closed his eyes. His face slackened and Webb tiptoed out of the room.

The mattress in his new bed was soft and lumpy; Webb ignored what normally would have bothered him. He rolled away from the light sneaking underneath the drawn shade. Exhausted, he fell into a series of dreams that seemed to be occurring at a considerable distance, almost out of sight. He watched himself perform as though looking at himself through the wrong end of a telescope. He sensed someone else, someone too small to see clearly. It might be a woman, the figure seemed soft with curves. He reached underneath his pillow and drew it tight against his cheek. His lips made pursing kissing movements. The image faded, he rolled onto his back, and began snoring loudly.

It was nearly dark when Webb awakened. He checked on Joe, who was sitting in the easy chair next to the open window. Circling his feet were a dozen soiled pieces of Kleenex.

"There's a perfectly decent wastebasket next to your bed," Webb said. As he bent down to pick up the tissues he felt a definite catch in his back. He had once spent a week in traction. "The mind heals," a professor had said. Optimist, Webb had thought. But sometimes it seemed to work. He made a point of not rubbing his back as he straightened up.

Joe's few possessions seemed to have multiplied. Everything he owned that was not hung in the closet was draped over the bed's headboard, the night stand, and the wheelchair. Even his three ties had slid from their hanger and lay curled up across his shoes like dozing snakes. Webb marveled at how little time it took Joe to make the room a complete shambles.

"The hospital kept straightening up, telling me a clean room would improve my mood. I told them I liked clutter. You don't mind, do you?"

"It's your room."

Balanced on the armrest of Joe's chair was an assortment of paperback books, a Time-Life book about World War II, and a glossy coffee-table edition of *Baseball's Greatest Heroes*. "One of the old volunteers gave it to me. Three days a week he would come and tell me how he saw Ruth point to center field. 'He did it for the kid,' the old man said. Sometimes I think I was the old man's therapy."

Joe coughed and wiped his mouth with a fresh Kleenex which he dropped at his feet. "Ooops. I'll try to remember." He started to bend forward from the waist, then stopped. "Just this once," he said to Webb as Webb picked up the soiled tissue.

"I'll get you an extra basket, one under each hand. It shouldn't be too much trouble, should it?"

"Heroes," Joe said. He held the book in his lap and pointed to Ty Cobb. "The guy filed his spikes so sharp they were like sliding knives. Chopped the infielders' hands and shins up real good. So they put him in the Hall of Fame.

Some fucking hero. Real heroes are the guys that stay home with the wife and kids, hang in there at some job they can't stand, because it's expected of them. A real hero is the guy who accepts the shit in life and doesn't complain."

"You serious?"

"Yeah. I've been thinking it over. I quit every decent job as soon as I was making some headway. Why? To show each boss that success didn't matter, that I could do without their petty stinking little jobs. But you know what? Those guys didn't care. They hated their jobs just as much. All they ever wanted from me was to make it easier for them. Twenty jobs, three wives, no kids. Here I am. Not a lot to show for it."

"You lived your life your own way. That's more than most can say."

"Second prize." Joe rolled his head against the back of the easy chair.

"It beats riding one job all the way to the bottom."

"I guess."

Next door Jessica began playing an up-tempo rendition of "Stella by Starlight." Joe tapped his slender, yellowed feet on the hardwood floor.

"She's beautiful, too," Webb said.

"You mean that's a woman playing?"

"I've been after her since she moved in."

"No problem. You've always had a way. Smooth talk, a flutter of the eyes, a sad woe-is-me look, a fake limp—I've never seen you at a loss for the right moves."

"She's different."

"You think she'd play for me?"

"No sooner said than done."

Webb walked next door. He stood and looked through the

wooden door. Jessica was at the piano, a studio upright jammed against the wall that joined their two cottages. The room was nearly dark and she was no more than a hazy shadow among the shadows. He had known many women, but none so intense and solitary. Most women he knew would have their doors bolted, windows fastened shut. They took courses in self-defense and carried Mace. Jessica sat in darkness with her door open, apparently oblivious. Did she live so much in the past that she thought it was still safe to walk the streets alone at night and leave her door unlocked?

Jessica swayed as she played. Webb imagined her body felt alive, joined to the music. By contrast, he felt stiff and unbending. He would have liked to dance across her living room floor, move to her music, but he stood motionless, resting against the doorjamb.

She played until the room was in complete darkness. Then she reached up to turn on a lamp next to the piano and saw Webb's shadow in the doorway.

"Yes?"

"It's me. Webb."

"I wondered how long it would be before you dropped over. Come on in and bring your sunny disposition with you." She motioned him to a love seat next to the piano. She flipped on the lamp.

It was a low-wattage bulb; he could barely make out her face.

"Is this when you hit me with the big pitch?"

"Would it work?" he asked.

"What's the pitch?"

"I've got a dying friend who'd like to hear you play."

"That's very good. You get an A for originality." Jessica

rose from the piano bench and sat down alongside Webb. "You want me very much, don't you?"

Webb nodded.

Jessica placed her hand gently on his. She ran her finger along the tendons of his hand, her eyes averted. "You won't interfere or presume?"

Webb shook his head.

"You realize that this might not be a good idea? I mean we're not exactly Mr. and Mrs. Stable." Jessica reached over and began to unbutton Webb's shirt.

He stopped her, holding her hand to his chest. "First you've got to play for my friend," Webb said.

"You're serious?"

"Unfortunately. An old buddy of mine moved in today. He's got cancer of the pancreas. He heard you playing; I promised him you'd play for him."

"Of course." Jessica dropped her hand to her lap.

Webb watched dust motes float in the dim light from the lamp. He looked away, the room suddenly darker by contrast. He turned back to the light; the motes were no longer visible. "Joe's stone broke, his wife's left him."

"Are you going to be able to manage? He'll need an attendant, or a nurse, won't he?"

"He doesn't want anyone. I guess I'm stuck."

Jessica moved closer to Webb, their thighs touching. "Bring him over. I'd like to meet your friend."

"Joe Walker," Webb said as he walked toward the door.

Webb rolled the wheelchair alongside Joe's easy chair. Joe waved him away. "I can still walk. Just give me your arm."

"Don't be ridiculous. You couldn't make it up the stairs this morning, what makes you think you can make it now?"

"I'm on my way to meet a beautiful woman. I don't need handicaps. Come on." Joe thrust his elbow towards Webb. "One hand will do."

The two men advanced slowly down the hallway and onto the porch. They started down the stairs. Joe's legs threatened to give way. Webb held him tightly, one arm around his waist, the other holding him by his belt. Joe gripped the wooden banister. The two men rested at the bottom of the stairs.

"It's another fifty feet. You got the strength?"

"More than you can imagine. Come on, soldier, we're nearing the end of the march." Joe started off under his own steam. He took a few long forceful strides, then his gait wavered. He made it to Jessica's front yard, where he held onto a metal fence post. Webb stood behind him, not helping. When he had regained his breath, Joe walked to the front door, which was still wide open. Jessica appeared. Without saying a word, she took Joe by the arm and led him to the love seat.

"You comfortable?" she asked as she fluffed a small pillow and slid it behind the small of his back.

"I've got a few bucks," Joe said.

Jessica laughed. "Any special requests?"

"Shouldn't we get acquainted first?" Joe smiled and stretched out as best he could. The seat was too short to allow him to lie down, and too rigid to permit him to slouch comfortably. His head rested on the wooden armrest. His slippers hung precariously from his thin feet, which dangled. Webb started to slide an extra pillow behind him. Joe gave him a harsh look.

Jessica played for a half hour. No one said a word. A few times Webb heard Joe humming.

Jessica finished, walked over to a brass floor lamp, and turned it on. Only then did Webb realize that Jessica had been playing in the same dim light she had been ready to make love in. She had not changed the mood to perform for a stranger.

Jessica turned to Joe. "Can you have a drink?"

"I'd love one, but I don't think my pancreas is in the mood."

"A little pot, then?"

"Now you're talking. You know, I have a vial full of THC, the pure stuff, in my medicine bag. It really does the job. But it's no fun by yourself. Joints are to share. THC still seems medicinal."

Jessica handed Joe a pipe, held a Bic lighter to the bowl while Joe inhaled. He coughed several times, but persisted, a cloud of smoke blurring his face. When he was finished, he offered the pipe to Webb.

"No, thanks."

Joe seemed surprised. "What's the matter? Cancer's not contagious."

"It's only my second day on the job. I've got to be on good behavior. Not any old clinic will hire you without checking to see if your license is still good."

Joe handed the pipe to Jessica, who took a deep draw, the bowl glowing red. She seemed nervous and fidgety, glancing at Joe without speaking.

"Cancer's tough to talk to," Joe said. "But don't worry. I make everyone nervous at first."

"It's not exactly that you make me nervous. It's more like feeling helpless." She took another hit, tossed her head back, held her breath, then slowly exhaled. "And small," she added. "Hold this," she said to Webb. She slid back onto the piano bench and played a quiet ballad that Webb recognized but could not name. She sighed with relief, grateful to wrap herself in song.

She was more frightened than Joe. Jessica hid behind her music, her passion for jazz a beautiful shield to cover her fears. Webb sensed she was emotionally fragile, perhaps had even been hospitalized. She played like a woman possessed. And maybe she was.

Have them choose an era, his old boss, Dr. Kimbrough, advised. Flapper, Fifties, Gay Nineties, classical Greek. Are they carrying historical novels? Gothics? How do they imagine themselves? Everyone has a period that shapes his life. Detect the midpoint of the time that should have been, for them. No point in bobbing a nose that wants to be aquiline. Get to the heart of their nostalgia and they will be yours.

Also, always remember: A man without a period to fall back on, to dream about, is like a man without a country. Maybe worse.

Jessica claimed the bebop era. Believing in the Charlie Parkers and Thelonius Monks and their tragic, misshaped, often shortened lives provided Jessica with background and direction. Bebop was the fiction of her life.

Webb had no such period.

He had first gone to New York when he was not quite seventeen. Insurance money from the car accident that took his parents partially paid for tuition at Columbia. A scholarship and odd jobs covered the rest. It had been his first time east of Reno. The bright lights and the sense of infinite possibility were overwhelming. He arrived a week before school began and traversed Manhattan in awe. Underneath he was frightened. He could disappear without being missed; worse yet, he could show up and not be noticed. The freedom of possibility.

After one year he transferred to UCLA, claiming it was cheaper, which it was. That wasn't the point. L.A. was home, even without any family. But the year in New York had stuck in his mind. From sunny California he decided that early sixties New York was to have been his period. But the years in the ambulance, an eyewitness to accidents and unexpected disease, had changed that.

Jessica was playing "My Funny Valentine." She inserted a chorus of "Autumn in New York," then looked over at him and smiled. Webb smiled back, dimly aware of the pipe in his hand and that he was stoned. For a brief moment he worried that he might not be able to manage alone in the clinic. Then he reminded himself of his present clientele. The Instantcare drop-ins of coughs, night sweats, headaches, and watery stools could be treated with his eyes closed.

During his residency Webb had met one plastic surgeon from Beverly Hills who had made a fortune taking off concentration camp numbers from forearms. Webb asked him how he could stand to do it, day in and day out. "They're just numbers, Dr. Smith. Sadness comes from the heart, from the blood, not from the skin. The epidermis is the only part of the body where mistakes can be erased. Tragedy is disease of the inaccessible parts."

Perhaps that explained Webb's choice of plastic surgery. It was a retreat from real sickness. To cover up the choice, there had been the nod-to-Hippocrates half-day a week in the cleft palate clinic.

Jessica launched into a slow blues. Joe clapped his hands softly in his lap, his dangling slippers swinging in a small arc, keeping their own semblance of time. He paused and rubbed his abdomen. He looked like he might be in pain, but it might be the pain of reminiscence. Webb hoped it was the latter. Pancreatic cancer worked by boring its way through the abdomen, through the nerves and bone.

Joe rested against the back of the couch. His eyes were half-closed. His fingers made tiny movements as though he were playing a tune on the air.

"Have you tried the cancer clinic in Tijuana?" Jessica asked. "They're supposed to have drugs unavailable here."

"I'd rather abandon hope than give in to quackery. Accepting a bum deal is one of the last triumphs left to modern man, and I do not wish to squander the opportunity on some greasy Mexican clinic." Joe leaned over and pulled on his slippers. "I'm just a little tired." He put his palm flat against the armrest and positioned himself to stand.

Jessica put her arm through Joe's and helped lift him from the couch. Webb took his other arm. He looked over at Jessica. Jessica shook her head and looked away.

"Save it for later," Joe said. "I think my pants are falling off." Jessica reached over and held his pants by a loop, while Webb tightened the belt. "Not too tight," Joe winced. "It's a tossup between squeezing the cancer and having my pants fall down. The ultimate comic dilemma."

After tucking Joe into bed, Webb went back to Jessica's. He still had over an hour before he was due at the clinic. He wasn't in the mood for sex, but felt that not showing up would put a strain in their relationship. He needn't have worried.

Jessica was sitting on a wooden chair at her kitchen table. Her elbows were on the table; she rested her chin in her cupped hands. She did not look up when Webb drew up a chair alongside her.

"He's no bigger than a bird. I can't think of a worse way to die," she said quietly.

Webb reached over and took a sip out of Jessica's glass. Scotch and water, no ice. It was warm and vaguely nauseating. Jessica took the glass from him and held it to her lips. She ran the rim of the glass back and forth, as though polishing her lower lip.

"One of my instructors at Juilliard had stomach cancer; he wasted away—one semester, start to finish. Is cancer of the pancreas the same?"

"He has a month, at most. Fluid's already beginning to accumulate in his lungs. His scans look horrible. The chemotherapy was worthless. The radiation just gave him diarrhea."

"You guys been good friends for a long time?" Her voice echoed in the glass.

"Yeah. It's like we can read each other's minds. Except that I don't know what he's thinking now. Or don't want to."

Webb stood up and walked to the sink counter, ran the water, filled a glass.

Jessica started to speak, then stopped and shook her head. She stood and walked over to Webb, who was still at the sink. She came up behind him and put her arms around his chest, her cheek against his back. She pressed her thighs against the back of his legs and slowly rocked. "I'm glad you're his friend," she whispered into Webb's shirt.

"I hope I'm up to it," Webb said.

"You will be. I can tell."

They walked into the living room, sat side by side on the love seat, shoulders touching, Webb occasionally running his finger along Jessica's thigh, tentatively, merely an announcement of his presence.

6

"**P**oint eighteen," Ray greeted Webb. "Nearly one in five that the world will come to an end."

"Please," Webb said to Ray. "We've got patients to see." He'd just finished his last garbage detail; finally, the community had been served. It was a relief to have that over with.

"We're in deep shit. You see those bombings in France. Those fanatic Iranian bastards are just toying with us. They've got uranium, they've got suitcases, what more do they need?" Ray wrung his hands and wiped them on his slightly soiled white duck pants. "It's getting really hot out there. It could be any moment now."

"Save it for your spare time. I have my own problems."

"That's the trouble with Western thinking. It's always from the inside out. First my problems, then we'll tackle the world, if there's any time left. Not a good attitude, Dr. Smith." Ray stuck out his chin and pushed a loose strand of red hair back behind his ear. Webb placed him in the sixties, complete with headband and mittfuls of beads.

Webb looked past Ray at the handful of patients gathered in the waiting room. "The afternoon shift too lazy to finish up?"

"Some drunk surfer nearly drowned, right at sunset. But Instantcare performed another medical miracle. They resuscitated him right on his surfboard." Ray's expression softened; he was happy to be distracted. "You should have seen Chief Williams. Good old Angel was in back, working over the books. He had the newspapers down here before the IV was taped to the armboard. 'It should be second page, minimum,' he's telling the reporter. 'Be sure to get the clinic sign as a caption,' he says. 'And the surfboard. Got to get a piece of the surfboard.' The photographer takes some pictures. Then Angel bends down and tells the man—who's still sputtering and coughing—that he hopes that the treatment at Instantcare was to his satisfaction. The doctors are standing around gawking, they're absolutely speechless." Ray looked out at the waiting room and laughed. "With all the excitement, I guess the afternoon crew left you the splinters and swollen piles."

Webb looked down at a mountain of tangled EKG paper lying on the counter. "This his?"

Ray nodded.

Webb read the tracing. "V fib. The real thing. He's a lucky man. Without our glorious quack-in-a-shack . . ." Webb made a slashing motion across his neck. "Thank God for free enterprise."

"One out of five cardiac arrests leaves the hospital alive—I read that in the paper. One out of five that the world will come to an end before the week is out. The coincidence of the statistics is curious. Maybe there's a correlation." Ray handed Webb the sign-in sheets for the waiting patients, and then slid into the three-wheeled burgundy upholstered chair behind the computer. He did some fast calculations. "I'll be here if you need me."

"Would you mind taking temperatures first? The end of the world can wait until we've seen the patients." Webb tried to speak with authority, but his heavy-lidded red eyes registered a lack of real power, as if he had been unplugged and was operating on a small auxiliary battery.

"No reason to get snotty." Ray rose, tucked a stethoscope and blood pressure cuff under his arm, and sauntered into the waiting room. "Help is on the way," he said to the handful of patients. "Yes, indeed, help is right here, at your disposal." Ray took the first of a series of blood pressures, at the same time looking over his shoulder at Webb, who was watching him through the glass sliding window separating the waiting room from the registration area.

Webb took each patient, in turn, into one of several small examining rooms off the main corridor. He removed a splinter, redressed an infected toe, ordered a pregnancy test, and took an EKG on a pizza overdose. He saved the hemorrhoid for last. The patient, a chubby, unshaven man in his middle forties, was bent over the tipped-up examining table. Webb, wearing a surgical mask, sucked in his own exhalations, smelling gauze, Cepacol, and stale pot. His breath reminded him of the foul morning odor of bars when they first open for business. It was the smell of blotted-out memories. With a gloved finger Webb examined the man's pouting anus: it resembled a tired brown flower. In the center was a cherry-red lump of tissue. "Thrombosed external hemorrhoid. We all get them. They hurt like hell, but there's nothing to worry about. If you want, I can make a little incision and the clot just pops out. It'll sting for a few days, but it's better than letting it go away on its own, which it will do, guaranteed."

"I'm afraid of needles," the man said into the pillow under his chin.

"You won't see a thing." Webb anesthetized the area, noting that this was not some Beverly Hills nose job or breast augmentation. What was it he had told Joe? That he had slid all the way to the bottom. Exactly. With his elbow Webb pushed a flap of the man's Marine World shirt out of his field of view. Just above the crease in the man's buttock a dolphin was jumping through a hoop. The dolphin was smiling. But what was he really thinking, Webb wondered as he made an elliptical incision and squeezed gently. Ray reached down and swabbed away the exposed clot with a handful of gauze pads.

"Want to show your wife?" he said with a laugh. "Tell her this is what a real pain-in-the-ass looks like."

"She already knows." The man gave out an embarrassed half-laugh, half-cough, relieved to be finished. Ray stepped on the pedal that tilted the table upright again. The man stood up, pulled up his pants, and thanked Webb profusely. Webb was annoyed at being thanked for something as trivial as fixing up a hemorrhoid. On the other hand, the man seemed more grateful than many of his former prima donna patients who took good looks for granted and shopped for new features with the same eye that they chose crystal and Wedgewood. He did not look the man in the eye, instead focusing on his own gloved hands.

"Your anus is still anesthetized. There will be a little

discomfort when it wears off. Take some hot soaks and try to keep the area clean."

"Thanks again, Doc." He turned to Ray and said, "Only in L.A. can you get your ass fixed in the middle of the night and be able to tell your old lady about it. Instantcare. I'll have to keep you guys in mind." The man walked out with a fake cowboy gait, his knees bent, his rear end pushed backwards. When he was outside on the street, his face a healthy pink in the glow of the Instantcare sign, he smiled, waved, and gave Webb the thumbs-up sign.

At one time Joe's cancer was smaller than this man's clot. And less painful. Tragedy is disease of the inaccessible parts. Webb moved to the sink, removed his mask and gloves, and washed his hands. He could smell soap, talcum powder, and the unpleasant sweetness of slightly aged blood. He had been unaware of it while operating, but now, with the clot double-wrapped and disposed of in a shiny steel waste bucket, the stench of blood was everywhere. Webb wondered if it was imaginary, or whether the molecules of olfaction were still clinging to the hairs inside his nose. He sniffed, but could not detect any difference. Either way, the odor was inside his brain. He felt mildly nauseous. "I'll be back in a minute," he said to Ray. He stepped outside into the night.

He had anticipated the cleansing effect of fresh air. Instead there was the fishy odor of low tide. The sky was low and heavy, as though compressed by a slowly collapsing universe. He stepped over a metal drain guard and onto the cool sand. He walked up over a small rise in the beach until he could see surf. Looking back, he could barely make out Ray sitting at his computer, calculating. Instantcare glowed like some low-wattage land lighthouse. The color was reminiscent of the purplish lights in meat markets and butcher shops. Most of the surrounding neighborhood was in bed; there was only the occasional flickering of late-night movies seen through darkened windows. The whole block reminded Webb of a cutout town that you could purchase with so many cereal box tops. Slip tab A into slot A, tab B into slot B, and you have a ready-made Main Street.

Webb squatted on his heels, facing the street. The surf carried on at his back, but Webb did not notice. The pot was wearing off, but he still felt removed and distant. Ray, motionless at his work, seemed like a toy add-on to a toy town.

Down on the street, Oblivion was unlit. On the second floor, behind a pulled shade, Milo slept. His wife dead for fifteen years, Milo kept on, dragging himself downstairs to serve drinks and listen to the passage of other lives. He had memories of New York, he had memories of his old life, when his wife was alive. The rest was filler. He had no children and nowhere to go. He came on the sheet of cardboard labeled "bar" and "bartender." Set the bartender up behind the bar, one hand on the beer spigot, the other on his hip. Put his bed upstairs. He will not be going anywhere.

Around the corner, two blocks up towards Canal Street, Jessica was asleep. Webb sniffed at the night air, wondering whether she would be wearing perfume. He knew so little about her. Perhaps that was part of the fascination. The old striptease of personality, a layer here, a layer there. Sometimes it seemed intentional and coy. Others he suspected some horrible pain covered over with layers of glossy diversion. He had asked her about her childhood and she had told him only that she had won a scholarship to music school. At her graduation recital, in the middle of the cadenza to a

Mozart sonata, she had slipped in the opening eight bars of "Ain't Misbehavin'," followed by a short improvisation, and back again to Mozart for the finish. She told him what the professor said, what the audience did, but never mentioned anything about her own feelings except to say that afterwards she laughed. Were her parents in the audience? Did she have family? What about the years after school and before now? Unimportant, she said. Mere biography, not the real thing. And what is the real thing? "*Moi,*" she'd say, pointing to her heart. "Sometimes."

Elizabeth had been a straight-shooter. There were no neuroses to skirt, no hidden agendas to sort through. Her biggest fault was that she had fallen for a man who had no sense of gratitude. Webb knew he should avoid comparisons between Elizabeth and Jessica. They would accomplish nothing except to remind him of what he had lost.

Next door Joe lay dying. The story of his future was the story of his past. He hoped he would be with him at the end. He did not want to walk into Joe's room and just find him.

Webb wrapped his arms around himself. There was the damp fragrance of chilly, wet sand. He heard someone hollering his name. He looked up to see Ray frantically waving at him. Webb jumped up and ran towards the clinic, away from his thoughts. He was glad to have a calling.

Ray was holding a four-year-old boy, stabbed through the cheek. The knife was still in place, the black wooden handle protruding just above the angle of his jaw. The cheek gaped open; there was surprisingly little bleeding, just a constant capillary ooze. While Ray showed Webb the wound, the boy held a bloodied towel to the side of his neck. With his other hand, he gripped the hem of his mother's soiled gray car coat.

She had her arm around his shoulder. Most of her nails were long and brightly painted—red with gold sparkles— but two were chewed short, the polish flecked and peeled. Her hand in the child's back fluttered uneasily, alternating between pats of comfort and aimless trembling. Occasionally she put her hand to the side of his neck, catching some of his tears on her finger. In the web of skin between her thumb and index finger was a crudely executed lavender cross. Above it a name had been written over, crosshatched into a rectangular purple anonymity. When she moved her hand back to the boy's shoulder, the tears ran into the boy's collar. The woman said little, carefully watching while Webb inspected the wound.

The plain handle was that of a steak knife, which meant serrated edges. Webb gently probed inside the boy's mouth. The boy started to cry but stopped, the pain of crying greater than the pain of the examination. Webb ran his finger along the inner cheek; he could feel the blade tip against the gum just above the incisors. He looked up at the woman.

"I told him he shouldn't be fooling with knives. He fell right on it," she said.

The boy looked up at his mother, as if to say something. The woman frowned and gave the boy a single hard sideways glance. Her jerky movements indicated uppers, probably speed and cocaine. The boy dropped his head.

Webb knew that the woman had stabbed her son.

He had seen more than his share of hookers and dealers at County, shrewd women who manipulated the staff, sweet-talked the doctors they could not intimidate, women who floated in and out of the hospital as if they owned it. Somehow they were able to make gonorrhea, pelvic inflammatory disease, and abscesses from dirty needles seem like sprained ankles—little unavoidable conditions without any social significance. If you questioned them, looked at them the wrong way, they accused you of not caring. If you said nothing they smiled and presumed they had gotten the best of you.

As a resident he'd been fascinated and repulsed. In practice he had operated on more than a few, mostly Medi-Cal referrals. Sometimes he thought he liked them, even admired them for their spunk and toughness of spirit. Sometimes he told himself that they were the real salt of the earth, in contrast to his well-heeled patients with their perfect attire and matching diction. Right now though, he saw the woman as a disgusting twenty-five-dollar-a-trick hooker with a drug problem and a four year old that she had stabbed through the cheek. He wanted to see her locked up.

"He needs to be in a hospital," Webb said. "We aren't set up for this type of . . . accident."

"You fix him. We've got money."

"They have all the proper equipment. He needs general anesthesia for the extraction of the knife, let alone the suturing."

"I can't take him there. We don't have a car."

"I'll call an ambulance." Webb started toward the phone.

The woman stepped in his way. "No hospitals. Booker's a good boy. You give him a shot, stitch him up, and we'll be on our way."

The woman stood between Webb and the door to the treatment room. She was broad-shouldered and powerfully built, though her legs were slender. She wore aquamarine high heels and tight shiny black pants. On her ankle was tattooed a pink flower. She pulled a wad of bills from a large, imitation leather shoulder bag and began counting. "This should cover it," she said, jerking her head slightly, not handing over the money, just standing in the doorway waiting for Webb's answer.

Ray read the woman's name from the registration papers. "Come on," he said. "We can give him a little nitrous and Demerol. Mrs. DeJohnette's right. They go to the hospital, the do-gooders will descend on her like the plague. They'd have to report her. It's state law."

The woman stuffed the money back inside her purse and folded her arms across her chest.

Webb stared at Ray and shook his head.

Ray bent down and looked Booker in the eye. The boy milked his mother's coat, his hand opening and closing, vacillating. He would not look directly at Ray. His eyes wandered the room, settling on a toy bear atop a medicine cabinet. Ray rose, walked to the cabinet, returned with the stuffed animal. The boy reached out, touched the bear's nose, ran his hand over the bear's face. Then suddenly he punched the bear as hard as he could, knocking it from Ray's hand. He kicked the bear, which skidded across the room and under the sink.

"I'll bet it hurts a lot," Ray said, his face only inches from Booker's.

Booker nodded and with his coat sleeve wiped some tears from his cheek. With his other arm he continued holding the bloody towel to his cheek.

"Whoever did this didn't mean it, did they?" Ray looked at Mrs. DeJohnette. "It was an accident, right?"

"Like I already told you. It was an accident. Booker's always playing where he shouldn't be. Never sleeps, always getting into something. If you got kids, you understand."

"I don't have kids. And I don't understand," Webb said. "It looks to me like someone stabbed Booker. He needs to be in the hospital. And this should be investigated."

"Easy," Ray said, grabbing Webb's forearm. "You ever lived in a foster home?" He walked over to Mrs. DeJohnette and looked into her eyes, studying her.

Mrs. DeJohnette held her ground, barely blinking. "I've been there. See what a good job they do?" She flashed Webb a tight smile, more of a sneer. "The only time you get hugged's when the welfare check arrives. County don't let me visit my daughter. I could buy her things, make her pretty. Better than cheap Sears and Roebuck shit three sizes too big, or so tight you can't breathe. But they don't tell me where she is."

"She's right," Ray said. "Foster homes are the worst."

"He's telling you like it is," Mrs. DeJohnette said to Webb. "Just fix my son and we're out of here." She put her hand on Booker's shoulder. "You're going to be okay. The doctor's going to make you all well again," she said, her voice now soft and comforting. "Then we'll go home and you can sleep in my bed. Just the two of us. You'd like that, wouldn't you?"

Booker tilted his head slightly so that his good cheek was resting against his mother's hand.

"I knew from the first moment that I saw you, that you'd be nothing but trouble," Webb said to Ray.

He did not have to treat the boy. This is a stupid idea, a no-win situation, he said to himself. Booker stood at his mother's side, quietly watching. Webb saw Ray and Mrs. DeJohnette looking at him. It wasn't fair. They had no right.

Ray approached the examining table, leading Booker by the hand.

"Thanks a lot," Webb said to Ray.

They lifted Booker onto the examining table, and eased him into position.

This is a zero-percentage proposition, Webb thought, as he spun the adjustable-height metal stool to its proper level. They catch you, you could go to jail. No license, some flaky broad who probably won't bring the kid back for follow-up.

From a supply drawer he took a pair of size eight gloves and dropped them on the stool. He couldn't wait to begin.

The boy's head rested on a blue pillow. Ray brought the overhead light around until it was focused on the wound. Webb looked up; the light was brilliant and momentarily fuzzed his vision. His thoughts jumped back to residency days at County Hospital, when he was in charge, in control. Legitimate. Webb shook his head and concentrated on Booker's wound. He realized that the boy's mother was standing over him. "Mrs. DeJohnette, perhaps it would be better if you waited in the other room."

She shook her head, squaring herself against the far side of the examining table, one hand resting lightly on Booker's forearm. She reached into her loose-fitting blouse and pulled out a large onyx cross which she held to her lips. Her eyes closed, she moved her lips silently, and then she dropped the cross back between her full breasts. "Let's get on with it."

Webb tried to place her accent; he guessed rural, maybe Arkansas or Oklahoma. Probably came to town by bus. Probably would leave the same way.

Ray brought out a mask and hooked it up to a fat green tank in the corner. "Take a few sniffs," he said to Booker, his hand cradling the boy's chin. "Then you won't feel a thing."

Booker's foot shot out, catching Webb in the elbow. There was a rush of pain up his arm. He glared down at Booker, at the same time forcefully grabbing his ankles. "Cut it out," Webb said. "It's for your own good."

Mrs. DeJohnette motioned him aside. She took over, holding both of Booker's ankles tightly in her grasp. Booker continued kicking; Mrs. DeJohnette held on. Then, with one forearm pressed across his thighs, she reached out and firmly took Booker's chin in her hand. She looked him in the eyes but did not speak. The boy's shoulders fell in resignation.

Ray brought the mask to Booker's face. His feet started up again. Mrs. DeJohnette shook the boy's chin ever so slightly; it was no more than a gentle vibration, but the boy winced and sunk back onto the table. Mrs. DeJohnette gave Ray a go-ahead nod. Moments later, Booker was quiet, his eyes glazed. Webb started an IV and injected a small quantity of morphine. Booker's respirations slowed and his hands fell open on the examining table. Ray manned the blood pressure cuff while Webb adjusted the height of the metal stool. He sat down and slipped on the gloves, enjoying the feel of silky talcum against his fingers. He settled forward on the stool, leaning into the boy, bracing one elbow on the table, and resting his other hand on the boy's neck. Webb was struck by the soft, perfect shape of Booker's ear. For a moment he sat tracing the outline of the small boy's jaw, as though he could actually palpate the beauty of innocence. At four there was still a glimmer of hope; by eight Booker would be streetwise, forever hardened; by ten he could be lifting car radios, peddling drugs. If caught, he would blame his childhood. And he would be right. Which would excuse nothing.

The scent of mildew rose from Booker's rough red-and-black checkered wool jacket.

Carefully Webb began to extract the knife. His hands were steady. The top of the blade appeared. It was serrated. Webb went even slower. He found himself humming. When doing cosmetic surgery he often wore headphones and listened to Bach or Vivaldi—he was especially fond of Vivaldi's "Glorias." He would turn up the music, the voices blocking outside sound, and imagine himself inside a soaring white cathedral with its single, great white light focusing directly down on him. At the conclusion of his surgeries, when he removed the headphones, he fully expected to hear applause.

He slid into "My Funny Valentine."

The pathway of the knife was millimeters from the parotid gland and the facial nerve. He met some resistance. He took his other hand, placed it inside Booker's mouth. A tooth of the blade was caught on one of Booker's molars. Webb hooked his own finger around the blade tip, and, using his fingernail, lifted the knife free. Booker jerked slightly but did not awaken.

Webb threw the knife across the room, into the sink.

Booker's mouth kept closing; Ray propped it open with a speculum normally used for pelvic exams. The boy coughed and turned his head a few degrees. Ray repositioned him, readjusting the light, aiming it through the aperture of the speculum so that Webb could see the extent of the laceration. Booker was fortunate; the knife's entrance had been just anterior to the junction of the posterior inner cheek and the side wall of his pharynx. The carotid artery, jugular vein, and the hypoglossal nerve had been spared. Webb sutured the mucosa, settling into the rhythm of his sewing. Briefly he wondered if he was still high, but it could just have been the pleasure of accomplishment.

The outer cheek took only minutes. The wound was slightly uneven because of the knife's serration. Webb trimmed the edges, then approximated them, fastened them with the finest cotton sutures Ray could find. The scar would be less than two inches in length. Finished, Webb leaned back on his stool, running his gloved finger along the neatly sutured wound. He noticed that Booker had on new sneakers, but that his pants were hand-me-downs, too big for his tiny legs, the cuffs triple-rolled.

He removed the sterile cloth drapes from beneath Booker's chin. Booker's pale face was streaked with Betadine. Webb took some alcohol swabs and wiped away most of the brown stain. There remained a pale tan perimeter. Webb brushed Booker's hair back off his forehead. A faint white line extended across the scalp line. This had not been the first time.

The woman had stabbed Booker. But he had no proof. Besides, who was he to judge? He remembered the hearing. They hadn't given him any chance to explain.

Mrs. DeJohnette stepped forward and inspected the wound. Her expression was all business as she examined Booker's cheek and the inside of his mouth. She looked up at Webb, her eyes dense and suspicious. For a brief second she relaxed, her drawn face revealing what might once have been a certain brittle attractiveness. "You're all right," she said to Webb. She started to smile, a thin red line broken by irregular darkened teeth, but changed her mind. With a single jerky movement she flipped open the clasp of her purse, its mouth falling open. Amid the clutter of packets of Kleenex, cosmetics, and a pack of Kools, Webb caught sight of a flat black pistol handle. Webb guessed the gun was small bore, maybe a twenty-two or twenty-five. He strained to see more.

Mrs. DeJohnette saw what Webb was looking at but made no attempt at concealment. She unzipped a side pocket of the purse, pulled out a wad of bills. Without asking the fee, she counted out one hundred forty dollars, in fives and tens, and slapped them in Webb's hand.

"This should do it," she said. Webb slid the bills into a cashbox in the top drawer of the intake desk. Ray wrote out a receipt and handed it to her.

"He's going to be sleepy for some time. Do you have any way to get him home?" Webb said.

"Get us a cab," she said to Ray, "and we'll be history."

"Make sure the boy takes these." Webb handed her a vial of antibiotics. "Mouth wounds are notorious for getting infected, so make sure he takes the whole bottle." Mrs. DeJohnette jammed the bottle into her coat pocket without looking at it. She would probably forget they were even there. "Don't forget," Webb said, but Mrs. DeJohnette was already opening the front door.

Ray carried Booker, who was still sleeping, to the cab. Webb stood at the window watching Mrs. DeJohnette slide in alongside Booker. The cab accelerated into the night.

The practice of clinic medicine was like a series of quick dances, a brief touching, before moving on to the next partner. He looked forward to seeing Booker again, though he could do without the mother. She would be nothing but trouble. He knew he shouldn't have treated Booker, not while his license was suspended. But he refused to consider the potential consequences. He walked back to the treatment room and scrubbed the talcum from beneath his nails. The stiff bristles of the nail brush were sharp against his fingers and brought back a sense of power, of what he could do, if he wanted.

"Nice job," Ray said, returning. "You have one first-rate touch."

"What'd you say today's number is?" Webb asked.

"Point eighteen."

"Funny, it doesn't feel that high."

7

Jessica was light against Webb's chest. A faint breeze came through the open window across from her bed. The room looked out on the back yard. Except for a cracked concrete birdbath standing just beyond the window, its bowl empty and iron-stained, the yard with its dusty shrubs and roses and faded tile patio could have been Webb's.

After they'd made love, Jessica flipped on a bedside portable cassette player and played a tape of Charlie Parker's 1954 recording of "What is This Thing Called Love." "Sorry about the poor recording," Jessica said. "Ignore the background hiss." Parker soloed while they listened. The tape finished. Jessica turned to Webb, and said softly, "Anyway, fidelity doesn't matter when you can play like that."

"I wouldn't know. I can't play like that."

"Did you really love your wife?"

"Yes."

"Milo says she's very beautiful."

"So are you. Besides, how would he know?"

"From her photo. Apparently every time you get loaded, you show him the same picture. You have it in your wallet?"

Webb reached over the edge of the bed, feeling for his pants. He found his wallet and slipped the picture out of the plastic jacket.

Jessica held the picture in her hand, then gave the photo back. Webb looked at it before sliding it into his wallet.

"You'd leave me in a second if you could get her back, wouldn't you?" Jessica propped herself on one elbow and looked him in the eye.

"Probably," Webb said.

"If you didn't, you'd be a fool." Jessica sipped from her wine glass. "It must be a good feeling, being settled. Not that I could stand it, mind you, but it might be . . . reassuring. Maybe someday I'll rent a marriage, try it out for a weekend. Something like that."

"I cheated on her."

"One-night stands or affairs?"

"Mostly one-nighters. Sometimes I didn't even know their names. I'd meet someone at a medical staff meeting, say some nursing supervisor, and we'd slip back to my office or to an on-call room. It was like an addiction."

"Sounds like you have a lot of respect for women."

"It had nothing to do with the women. I can't even blame it on a wife who didn't understand me. Quite the contrary. It was like I couldn't help myself. I think I wanted to get caught."

"Why?"

"I'm not sure. Guilt, desire for self-destruction, pure arrogance, a feeling of being above judgment. Now I wish I hadn't."

"The day I left for California I burned everything: old photos, letters, even my grammar school report cards. You know what was left? A few ounces of black ashes. Which I dumped out the window. My past scattered to the wind. Poetic, don't you think?" Jessica asked.

"No, I don't. If there's something horrible in your past I'd rather know it. I'm not in the mood to have an affair with a dream. I need someone solid."

"What if what you found out scared you away?" Jessica sat up and dangled her legs over the side of the bed, her back to Webb. "What if it scared me away?"

"Have you tried counseling, therapy?"

"You think I got this way all by myself? No, sir. I've had plenty of professional guidance. The best, so I've been told. I guess psychiatrists are like baseball players: even the stars sometimes get in a slump. You might call me a bad season."

"Is it that hard to talk straight, without making jokes?"

"I wasn't making a joke." Jessica continued looking out the window. She squeezed her hands tightly in her lap. "Three times a week, years on end, the little shit doctor saying, 'and.' Like I could cough up my troubles into a Kleenex and hand it to him. There's always more, until you feel completely drained. And then there's still more. But it doesn't make any difference. As long as I can play the way I want."

"You don't mean that."

"Yes, I do. No matter how bad they make it, they can never take away your music. So that's what counts, what's left behind that is yours, and yours only."

"What really happened?"

Jessica shrugged.

"You said you'd level with me."

"There never was any recital. At least not a second half. I couldn't finish. I froze."

"That could happen to anyone," Webb said.

"Once. Not every time."

"You play at Oblivion."

"Yeah, I've got some audience over there. Oblivion's not Carnegie Hall."

"And that's it?" Webb asked.

"You want more? Well, stick around. But not today." Jessica reached out and stroked Webb's hand. "I read that Monk would get so far out on his solos that the players in his rhythm section would fold their hands, sit back, and wait. They knew it was a matter of time before the melody returned. He just had to wander off to get a new view of an old tune. Maybe I like you because we're both trying to take a fresh look." Jessica slid over to Webb and wrapped both arms around his neck. She tucked her head under his chin. "And because I think you're a good man."

Webb's voice was soft against her hair. "I want to know more."

It was late afternoon. Early fall shadows spread along the dusty gravel path leading to Webb's cottage. One of the barrel cactus plants next to the front steps was in bloom: a fragile white flower emerging between the sharp spines. This was the wrong season for blossoms. He smiled at the cactus, which looked as if it enjoyed defying nature. If a dirty cactus can do it, so can I. He took the front steps two at a time, thinking that he might give them a fresh coat of paint.

"I hope you're nicer to her than you've been to the others," Joe said. He was slumped in the front room easy chair. The chair was a greenish yellow, streaked by the sun, with worn areas on both armrests, the pattern rubbed smooth by years of elbows. A magazine lay open on Joe's lap. In his blue VA robe, open at the knee, Joe was the picture of domesticity. All he needed was a beer.

"Kiss my ass," Webb said. He patted Joe on the thigh as he moved through to the kitchen. The feel of his friend's wasted flesh dampened his mood. I'm getting laid while Joe is getting fucked, he thought. He pulled two Budweisers from the fridge. From the kitchen window he could see Jessica's bathroom window. The light went on. Was she washing herself? Would she be thinking of him as she wiped him away? A strange woman, but he had known this all along. A woman of her talent playing for doughnuts and coffee at some two-bit bar for the fallen. And it wasn't just a fear of playing in public. Concert pianist and plastic surgeon, now just two pieces of flotsam washed up by the daily tide.

He uncapped the two bottles as he walked the short hall-way to the front room.

"Thanks. The alcohol will probably kill me, but this way it seems more like an ordinary afternoon. And believe me, at this stage of my life, habits are worth dying over." Joe took a deep swallow, then another, let out a small belch, and wiped his mouth on the sleeve of his robe. "No big deal, but I prefer Heineken's. Budweiser reminds me of bowling, tastes like someone dropped talcum in the bottle."

"Aren't we choosy." Webb dropped onto a couch across

the room, his feet on the far edge of the oval chocolate-brown throw rug that took up most of the center of the living room.

"Nice place you got here. Decorate it yourself?" Joe picked at a loose thread hanging from the easy chair.

"It's rented. Furniture, toilet paper, everything. And don't be smart. Early whorehouse seems about right for my circumstances."

"Were you high-tech when you had money?"

"How'd you guess?"

"You don't look much like antiques and precious porcelain. Of course, I'd never know. You never had me over."

"A difference of wives. There was no point. Besides, you didn't miss anything. A stereo, a couple of chrome lamps, and a few leather chairs."

"I missed coming over and being uncomfortable."

"Yeah. Success didn't make me much of a friend."

"But that's past now." Joe finished his beer, hoisted the bottle to Webb.

"Like old times," Webb said. He went to the kitchen and brought back a cold six-pack.

"Things working out okay at the clinic?"

"Sure. It's nothing but first aid and basic psychiatry. I don't know how many more headaches I will be able to hear about, but for the moment it feels good to have a job. And, I must confess, it's a little bit of all right to have someone call me Doctor."

"Get them to give you back your license. You could use the clinic as evidence that you are capable of the straight life."

"Catch-22. I'm suspended."

"You have friends. They could stand up for you."

"Like at the hearing? You'd have thought I had leprosy."

"Keep at it. Eventually the medical board or whoever gives back the licenses will have to listen."

"It must be nice to be so filled with confidence."

"There's no point in anything else. Cynicism is for the healthy. I'm even thinking of taking up prayer."

"If you think you're being heard, say one for me."

Webb and Joe simultaneously took a swallow from their bottles. In the distance a motorcycle started up. The two men listened until the bike was out of hearing range.

Joe living with him was okay now. But Webb hated to think of how much work there would be later, when Joe was sicker. It would be easier if he could hire someone, but neither of them had the money. And Joe insisted that he did not want some woman from the nurse's registry hanging around trying to make him feel better. And he didn't want any male nurse touching him. He could be very demanding, Webb thought, finding himself mildly irritated to see Joe just sitting in his chair, drinking his beer, as if he didn't have a care in the world.

Webb broke the silence. "This guy goes to the doctor and finds out he only has twelve hours to live. He runs home and tells his wife. 'Come on, we'll go to the best restaurant, have the finest wines, get loaded, go dancing, then come home and make love all night.' 'That's easy for you to say,' his wife says, 'you don't have to get up in the morning.'"

"Do me a favor. Not too many jokes about the man who only has a day to live—'Move to Philadelphia, it'll seem like forever.' It gets a little old."

"Sorry." Webb hoped he hadn't told the story intentionally to be cruel.

He slouched on the couch until his body was at the same

angle as Joe's. He let out a soft laugh. "We look like a matched set."

"Not quite."

The afternoon bumbled to an end, the shadows lengthening, the room sliding into darkness. Webb listened to Joe's gentle snoring and what sounded like "These Foolish Things" coming from next door.

It was dark when Webb awakened with his hand asleep, crushed between his cheek and the poorly padded backrest. "Time for bed," he said to Joe. "I think you've had enough for one day." As Webb helped him back to bed, Joe mumbled something that Webb could not make out. Joe was heavier than he had been earlier in the day. Maybe it was the beer, maybe it was the burden. It would be easier to use the wheelchair, even inside the house. But Joe insisted on walking.

Webb felt a stab of pain in his back and down his left leg. It was the old sciatica acting up.

"See you tomorrow," Webb said. He tucked Joe in. Joe mumbled again. As Webb turned to leave, he was struck by the solitariness of the two pair of shoes on the closet floor. He recognized the denim sneakers that Joe wore to the track. The others were a pair of brown wing-tips, from the days when Joe had sold insurance. That they would be enough, that Joe would never need to buy another pair, or even go to a shoe repair store, suddenly frightened Webb.

There were no boxes of souvenirs, photographs, or even cancelled checks or IRS returns. Everything Joe owned was either at his bedside or hanging in the half-empty tiny closet. It wouldn't take more than a half hour to clear up after he was gone.

Webb took a Valium from Joe's bedstand, turned out the

light, and went to his own room. He debated taking the pill, holding the yellow tablet in the palm of his hand. Just this once. A single Valium was no big deal.

He lay back and waited for the pill to take effect.

A tattoo reading JESUS LOVES was sliced in half, JESUS and LOVES now separated by an oozing gash. Webb pulled the edges back slightly and the bleeding increased. None of the slashes had nicked a tendon; though red and angry, they were all superficial. The man held his arm away from his body and looked at it as though it were someone else's. "I bleed, therefore I exist," he said to Webb. His voice was calm, as though he were indifferent to the slow dripping of his blood onto the tile floor of the examining room. His eyes gave him away, great, wide terrified eyes that did not blink, that darted from his wound to Webb and back again.

"Drugs?" Webb said to Ray, who only shrugged and held the man's shoulders against the table.

"See, red blood. From the heart. Down the little arteries, through the capillaries, then out the veins, onto the floor. Watch." He raised his eyebrows, then squinted. He reached over towards the lacerated lower forearm, but Ray caught his hand and held it to his side.

"The boss needs a clean field," Ray said, glancing at the man's sign-in papers. "Dave, right?"

"Dave, slave, man without a country, bounty, Dave is the name."

"You been depressed?" Ray asked, one hand still holding Dave's, with the other readjusting the drapes over the wound. Webb was anesthetizing, and then exploring.

"Do I look depressed? Morose? Worried? Concerned?

Hopeless? Anxious? Profound? Illiquid? Penitent? Take your pick. One of the above. Give you a clue. Guess penitent. Hey, you're fucking hurting me." He struggled against Ray's grip, but did not move the injured hand, which was firmly secured to an armboard by two Velcro straps fastened beneath the table.

"Easy does it. A few stitches and we'll get the bleeding stopped," Webb said. He worked quickly in a rhythm born of years of practice. "Then you can go over to County and have them sew up your psyche."

"That's not very funny," Ray said.

"You gonna save my life or just prolong it?" the man said to Webb. "'Cause if you're going to save it, I'd like to take a picture. A Polaroid, if you please." The man's feet were going underneath the wool blanket. Webb noticed that the man was wearing expensive, soft leather tasseled loafers and argyle socks. This was a man who spent time choosing his clothes. Webb had always associated expensive shoes with self-control and a precise sense of direction. Of course, he knew better.

"Neither. The cut's mainly soft tissue." Webb patted the man's hand.

"Soft tissue. Like my mind. Gray matter that doesn't matter."

Ray wrote down the number of the neighborhood Crisis Clinic. "Give them a call," he said as he tucked the folded piece of paper in the man's shirt pocket.

"Don't need no help. Need God. Need salvation. Need the Immaculate Conception or at least a small miracle. A vision, if you please. Right here in River City."

Webb sutured up the last flap of skin. It would leave marks, a telltale razor-thin row of scars marching up his arm. Tattoos of despair. Ultimately just a thin white grid of hurt. Webb wrapped the forearm and wrist in gauze. He told Ray to let the man up. Ray released his grip slowly, at the same time easing the man into an upright position. For the first time Webb looked directly at his face. He was an ordinary man in his late twenties. He reminded Webb of a cartoon of a man under x-ray who can be seen to have a single tightly-coiled spring where his vital organs normally would be. That was the first frame. The second frame would show the spring snapping, the man's eyes crossing, and some harebrained caption that's supposed to be funny. And never is.

"Thanks," the man said, only momentarily subdued. "Nice work if you can get it, and you can get it anytime." He winked at Webb. "I think I'll be going now. Got places to visit, people to see, taxes to pay, meters to pay, policies to pay, get a toupee, that sort of thing. Too long a line at County. Besides I've got insurance. Work for insurance. Term versus life, take your pick. Company policy, double indemnity if I kill myself on the job."

He reached into his wallet and pulled out an assortment of credit cards, parking stubs, business cards, and, finally, his laminated insurance card.

The man handed his card to Ray. "I'm okay."

"You have a place to stay?" Ray asked.

The man nodded.

"And you'll stay out of trouble."

The man nodded again.

Ray did the necessary paper work, then handed the man his copy. "Send this to your insurance company in the morning," he said, pointing to the yellow sheet, "and keep the pink copy for your records."

"Yeah, yeah. Yellow in the mail. Pink for my records. Got it. You two have been very kind. Maybe in the next life I'll be able to return the favor." He started to fold the papers, then wadded them up and threw them in a nearby wastebasket.

"You sure you're going to be all right?" Ray said.

"Got to go now. Need plenty of sleep. Early bird catches the worm." The man slid off the examining table and, with his good hand, brushed himself off. He slipped his tie back into position, straightened his back, and left.

"A couple hours ago he probably was selling someone a policy. Then . . ." Webb snapped his fingers. "And tomorrow, maybe he'll be back at work, telling his friends that he fell on a broken glass. Or he won't be back at work, he'll be incoherent at a baseball game, or singing accompaniment to some guitarist out on the dunes." Webb stared out at the darkness beyond the Instantcare sign.

"By the way, please don't keep telling the patients they'd be better off at County," Ray said. "I'd rather go to an animal hospital than spend one second in that shit hole." He lifted up his shirt. An irregular foot-long scar outlined his lower rib cage. "They let a third-year medical student stick in a chest tube. I suppose the staff physician thought it would be a good experience for the medical student, in case they ever got a real patient."

"Overall they give good care. I ought to know, I spent a third of my training there."

"Lots of good material, right?"

"Yeah. Wards chock-full of guinea pigs."

Webb had heard the accusations about County a thousand times. Any moment Ray would launch into a diatribe on impersonal public medicine, the long waits in the emergency room, the lack of supervision, and the constant foul-ups. Of course it was all true, and yet it wasn't the whole picture. He could not honestly say that the care was worse than the average for private practice. Clinical staff from the community and the university did review the tough cases. He had a sense of affection for County and blood-and-guts medicine: major trauma, gunshot wounds, massive burns, limb reconstruction. It was the civilian equivalent of war medicine.

He had turned down a full-time job there as attending in plastic surgery. He was going to make his mark in private practice and be a big shot. Now a job at County sounded like a permanent position in paradise.

"You try spending a year on the pediatric TB ward when you're only five, and see how well you like it." Ray glared. "Anyway, we need to meet the quota. Otherwise old Williams'll kick our asses off this gravy train."

"I think we've exhausted this line of conversation." Webb threw his gloves in a metal wastebasket. He opened the treatment room door and looked out at the empty waiting area. "I'm going upstairs to take a nap."

He dropped onto the narrow bed. The room was stark, holding only a bed, a desk, a goose-neck lamp, and an intercom. He turned out the light and curled up facing the wall, his feet tucked beneath a tightly folded blanket at the foot of the bed. He was still wearing his shoes; he felt more comfortable sleeping in a state of preparedness. He told himself it was in case there was an emergency downstairs, but he knew differently. Since his paramedic days, he'd often slept with his socks on, particularly when he was having a series of nightmares. He had explained to Elizabeth that it was poor circulation.

He did not wear them when he slipped out on Elizabeth.

He'd often slept better in strange beds than in his own extra-firm orthopedic bed at home. As long as he was with a new woman. Once he was comfortable in the relationship, his insomnia returned. He found the irony vaguely amusing: exciting women put him to sleep.

After a half hour Ray buzzed on the intercom. "You'd better get on down here."

Wheezing was audible from the foot of the stairs. An old man in a shiny, fifties-style double-breasted suit sat hunched over in a waiting room chair. He wore ancient cracked leather slippers. Underneath his coat was a striped pajama top. His wife, wrapped in a black wool coat that hung nearly to her ankles, stood at the reception desk, clutching her purse.

"What's the matter?" Webb asked his wife.

"He can't breathe. It's been an hour. The cab didn't come. We called another. They both came at the same time. One of them got mad at me. He had no right. Make him better," she said, motioning to her husband. Her hands were shaking. "Please."

Webb and Ray eased the man into a wheelchair, rolled him to the treatment room, and lifted him onto the examining table. His ankles were puffy; there was blueness around his lips. "Ever happen before?" Webb asked.

The man shook his head. He started to talk, but it was too much effort. The strap muscles of his neck stood out as tight cords. There was a white stubble of beard under his chin.

"You take medicines?"

The man nodded.

"Which ones?"

He shook his head and motioned to his wife, who stood behind Ray, balancing herself with one hand on the edge of the sink. She looked puzzled; she opened her purse, groped inside, closed it again. She shrugged her shoulders.

"You have a regular doctor?"

"We tried, but he's away till Monday. The other doctor doesn't know us."

"Do you have any idea what type of pills you take?" Webb asked them both. "Heart pills? Blood pressure pills?"

"Maybe heart. I'm not sure. They're small yellow ones." The woman held up her thumb and index finger and indicated the pills were tiny, as if to say that they didn't count for much. "Yellow," she repeated. She glanced at her husband, and then at Webb. "He never remembers anything," she said.

The man's hands were clammy, the nail beds blue. Webb and Ray helped the man out of his jacket. His pajama top was worn and damp. Webb unbuttoned it, eased the man's arms out, one at a time. He started to listen to his chest, but the woman grabbed him by the arm.

Webb put his other hand on hers, which was still gripping his forearm. "He'll be okay. Why don't you have a seat?" But the woman did not move. Now she was gripping her husband's hand, alternately squeezing and patting. Webb leaned around her, listened to the man's heart and lungs, the wheezing louder and more insistent. Ray eased the man back on the table, angled at forty-five degrees to allow him to breathe more easily. He ran an EKG strip. Webb read it as the paper flowed from the machine. Ray watched over Webb's shoulder.

"Looks like a U wave," Ray said. "And atrial flutter. Right?"

"Next thing you'll be telling me you do open-heart surgery on weekends," Webb said to Ray. "Big deal. You can read an EKG."

Ray turned his back and walked to the medicine cabinet where he drew some fluid up into a syringe. Then he took a second vial and prepared an additional syringe. He held them in his hand while Webb questioned the woman.

"Does he normally take potassium?" Webb asked. The husband and wife looked at each other quizzically. They were old, perhaps in their eighties. They had no idea what medicines they took, nor why. "Potassium," Webb said. "A red liquid."

"What?" she asked, cupping her hand to her ear.

"Potassium. A red liquid."

"A teaspoonful twice a day?" the wife asked.

Webb nodded.

"We ran out last week. I was going to get it refilled. I really was. I guess it slipped my mind." She started to cry. The old man reached out and held his wife's hand. Then he closed his eyes, his hand still resting on his wife's. "I have to do everything," the woman said. "Sometimes I forget." Her voice was muffled. She dried her tears with a wrinkled piece of Kleenex she pulled from her sleeve.

Webb started an IV. "We'll need some potassium," he said to Ray.

"Forty milliequivalents per cc. Ten cc's." He handed Webb one of the syringes that he had already prepared. Webb injected the potassium through the rubber top of the bottle of dextrose and sugar.

"Okay. What else?" Webb put his hands on his hips and stared at Ray.

"Lasix," Ray said. He handed Webb the other syringe.

"Nowadays everyone thinks he's a doctor," Webb said to the woman who was looking admiringly at Ray. Webb secured the IV tubing with some adhesive tape. It was strictly cookbook medicine. Read one manual and you could take care of most general medical problems. Put a decent self-help section in the back of the phone book, one with good pictures and large print and you could eliminate 90 percent of general practitioners. Include a cassette that would say that you were going to get better. The cassette with its perfectly modulated, soothing voice, perhaps accompanied by New Age music to meditate by, would certainly be better than most rushed doctors. And you could play it over and over without being charged for the follow-up visits. All that was left for Webb to do now was to adjust the number of drops per minute. Four years of general surgery residency and three more in plastic surgery and he was reduced to counting the number of drops coming down the tubing.

The rhythm shifted to a slow atrial flutter: 120 to 130. The wheezing lessened. Webb stood back and watched the woman watching her husband. For the first time he noticed that she wore open-toed shoes and that her legs were also swollen. He walked to the other side of the examining room, picked up a stool, and slid it beneath her. He stood behind her, his hands on her shoulder.

"He'll be feeling better any minute now," he said softly, bending slightly, aiming his voice at her ear. He could feel her body tremble. "We'll just let him rest here." He ran another EKG strip. The rate was now 100. The man's eyes were still closed; he began to quietly snore. Webb walked to the wall switch and turned off the bright overhead light. He dimmed the recessed lighting before he stepped out into the reception area.

He was nothing more than a plumber or a carpenter. Ray could manage almost any patient they were likely to see at the clinic. Once he dreamed of being special; now he couldn't be more ordinary. There was no point in kidding himself. He was past starting any new career. Getting started in plastic surgery again would be nearly impossible. He would work the clinics, be on a par with the nurses and aides.

Except for cases like Booker. Not everyone knew the anatomy and how to avoid complications. That was why you took a seven-year residency. The head of the department of plastic surgery had told Webb on the final day of his residency that he was one of the best the university had trained. A pretty long fall.

He wanted to see Booker again, if only to take out the sutures and see how the wound was healing.

Elizabeth had wanted kids. Webb had said to wait until he was financially established. Now he thought of the innocent beauty of Booker, his tiny Keds under the examining table, his large brown eyes watching him. Webb was filled with longing to pick Booker up and press him tightly against his chest. But he wouldn't. Booker wasn't his child. He had no claims.

There was another patient to be seen. Webb took him into a smaller examining room at the rear of the clinic. A simple strep throat, it took only minutes. When he returned to the main examining room both the husband and wife were asleep, the woman's head lying on the edge of the examining table, supported by her arm. The top of her head pressed against her husband's rib cage, her white hair flowing from the joining like water from a fountain. Her other arm was outstretched, her hand palm up over her husband's heart. Webb guessed the man's rhythm at about 100 by watching her hand flutter on his chest. He was careful not to make any noise as he left the room.

119

They slept until the end of his shift when Webb went in and shook the woman gently by the shoulder. She lifted her head, gave Webb a curious startled look, gathering her senses. Her husband was still snoring. She abruptly reached over and shook him by the chin. He snorted, opened an eye. She leaned over and kissed him on the lips. She turned to Webb.

"We can leave? He's all right?"

"He can go if you promise to take him to his regular doctor. Today. He needs his medicines checked. He might need something else."

Ray entered the room and offered to help the man back into his clothes. "That's not necessary," she said. "We can manage." The old man dangled his legs over the examining table edge while his wife slipped him back into his pajama top and his jacket. She squared his slippers on his feet. The man stepped onto the floor, steadied himself, took a few short steps going nowhere. She took his arm. "Step," she said sharply. "Lift your feet."

The man's feet marked time, inching forward, moving into short, but manageable steps. He headed toward the door, guided by his wife's light touch on his elbow. He stopped in the doorway, turned to Webb and nodded. The man opened his mouth, murmured something that Webb could not understand. Webb realized that he had never heard the man speak.

"He said 'Thanks,'" his wife said.

They were still in the reception area, waiting for a taxi, when Webb went off duty. Standing outside the clinic, in the bleached gray morning light, he could see them sitting, side by side, staring out the window. They were holding hands.

8

"**Y**ou lose, you double up. You win, you draw back part of the money, let the rest ride. It's a cinch. It'd be like going out in the yard and picking the biggest flowers." Joe sat in the easy chair facing the small rear yard with its cluster of scraggly untended rosebushes. He rested his elbows on the battered windowsill. His back was supported by two orange pillows. Webb disliked rosebushes. Reach for beauty and prick your finger. God's little joke. He stood next to Joe, looking instead at the sky: a brilliant blue, not a cloud in sight. The blue was mere reflection, an illusion. Space is black as night; the sky is black, not blue.

He could not accept Joe's condition. If he had read about it in the newspaper—an airplane accident or a drowning— it would have been immediate, and somehow tolerable. Joe would be gone, but he would not have gone through the process of dying. He recalled the space shuttle catastrophe, the astronauts blowing up over and over again in slow motion, on every TV screen in America. Everyone looking at the replay, trying to determine whether or not their deaths had been instantaneous, or whether they had lived long enough to know. The lower right-hand corner of the screen had counted the seconds, the tenths of a second from the explosion until the fragments disappeared into the ocean. At most they could have been alive for two minutes, one reporter said, knowing the audience was measuring in its mind how much suffering would be acceptable. A NASA official spoke quietly, looking directly into the camera, and said that their deaths must have been immediate, and he cited statistics on heat and the force of the explosion.

Joe had been sick for six months. He did not need to count in milliseconds.

He had weighed two-sixty, minimum. His shirts always pulled at the buttons, as though he were having a private tug-of-war between his parts. He had possessed an excess of flesh and spirit. Now he was yellow skin and white bone. His sclera were tinged with the same bile color that was rising in his blood. Webb rested his hand on Joe's shoulder and felt a hollowing out, his very shape marginally held together by marrowless bone, the man's scapulae brittle, grounded wings that could only tremble and shudder but could not move the stale air that surrounded him.

It was a sweet, rotting smell. Webb ignored it as best he could. He was careful not to be conspicuous about opening the windows. He did not sniff. He was thankful that olfaction adapts. This he had learned in the ambulance, relearned with cadavers, autopsies. Sometimes he wondered if Joe's smell was real, or if it was just what Webb had come to expect. As a kid he had avoided getting close to dead animals. He would walk to the opposite side of the sidewalk to avoid a splattered pigeon. Then it was the County ambulance and flesh was backdrop. Fragrances were memories, odors were bitter reminders.

Webb tried to smooth back Joe's cowlick, a clump of thick brown hair that refused to lie down. The hair popped up as soon as Webb withdrew his hand. "The system never works," Webb said.

"Sure it will. We'll start with small bets, say one or two dollars. Each time we lose, we double up. Two, four, eight, sixteen, thirty-two, sixty-four, one twenty-eight, two fifty-six, five-twelve. Let's see," Joe said, counting on his fingers. "That's nine bets. Surely we'll win one out of nine. If not, we can always bet one thousand, then two thousand. Sooner or later, we'll be bound to win."

"Where are you going to get that kind of money?"

"Borrow it from you."

"I'm as busted as you are."

"Get an advance on your salary."

"Impossible. I just started."

"All the better. The clinic needs some real talent. Surely this guy Williams will lend you a few hundred. Make it a thousand, even."

"The system doesn't work. They don't let you bet more than two hundred at a two-dollar table. That means that you lose eight times, you're finished."

"Wrong. They'll let me bet as much as I want."

"No, Joe. I've been there. There are house rules."

"Not for the dying. Let's say, speaking hypothetically, that I lose eight times, well then, you step up to the pit boss and say that your friend is dying. You think they're going to refuse me another bet or two? These casinos work on good word-of-mouth. What would be better than relaxing the rules for cancer? I'm telling you we can't lose."

"We don't have the money and we can very definitely lose. I'm not going into debt over a system that's a proven failure."

"They let dying kids go to Disneyland. What's wrong with a little shot at Vegas? Come on, it'd be a gas. You could push me from casino to casino and feel like a big shot. The women would fall all over you. Imagine the sentimental appeal: defrocked doctor helps dying friend break the bank."

"You're serious, aren't you?"

"You don't think I'm going out without a little fling? We book a two-night, three-day package, we go gamble and drink, I take little naps, we find a hooker who wants to sit on Death's face. Then I come back and die, peaceful and quiet-like, no complaints, no 'Fuck you, God,' no bitterness. I wrap myself up in the memories of a solid weekend with my buddy, slip off like a good old tired dog."

"I'll see if I can get the money." Webb squinted into the afternoon sun pouring through the greasy window. "Now let's both take a Valium and get some sleep."

"**Y**ou gave him the pills, all of them?" Webb said to Mrs. DeJohnette, though he already knew the answer. Booker's cheek was swollen and red, the wound ragged and weeping, the skin beneath the black sutures puckered and raw. Booker flinched as Webb squeezed lightly; a small drop of pus oozed from the corner of the wound.

"Sure," Mrs. DeJohnette said. Her voice jabbed and defended. "Just like you prescribed."

"He needs antibiotics; he needs to go to the hospital where they can administer IV's."

"No." She took Booker by the shoulder and aimed him at the door. "We'll find another doctor." The boy squeezed his mother's hand and looked bewildered.

"Call the ambulance," Webb said to Ray.

Mrs. DeJohnette opened the door, her other hand resting lightly at the back of Booker's neck. Her nails were lacquered ebony, except for the little finger, which was done in a glittery silver, matching the broad rings on each finger. She guided her son outside, and walked to the curb, checking for a cab. Booker sat on the edge of the curb, head down, bracing himself with his arms extended behind him, his palms flat on the sidewalk. It was after 2:00 A.M. Oblivion was closed, the street empty. It might be hours before a cab passed. Webb watched as the woman paced under the clinic sign, imagining the staccato clicking of her spiked heels against the pavement.

Ray stepped out into the purple light. "Come on, Booker. Let's get you cleaned up." Booker hesitated, staring at Webb, who was still watching from the waiting room. Reluctantly Booker took Ray's outstretched hand and followed Ray inside, to the nearest examining room. The two of them stood alongside the examining table, holding hands, waiting for Webb.

Mrs. DeJohnette walked up to Webb and grabbed him by the forearm. "Don't waste your time thinking about making any phone calls. The county took my little girl. They're not getting Booker. Think of the trouble you'd have explaining why you didn't send him there in the beginning. So you be a good doctor and get in there and fix up my son."

"Just answer me one question. Why didn't you give him the pills?"

Webb knew the woman was going to lie. He knew he should have refused to take care of the kid the first time. His was a lifetime of acting for concealed but shabby motives. Probably he had only operated on Booker so that he could tell Milo not to tell Jessica. Now it was too late to send the boy to County. If he did they might find out he was practicing without a license.

The word *inexorable* came to mind. A free man was a man with choices. He was definitely not free. She had him, and she knew it. You could see it in the way she was staring at him.

She stood in the doorway, only inches from Webb. In the purple light her hair flamed and flew into the night. Her eyes huddled deep in their sockets, giving away nothing, coldly scrutinizing him from a great distance. She ran her index finger back and forth across her thumbnail, stripping away a sliver of nail polish. She bit her lip before speaking. "He was doing fine. I made a mistake, okay? Is that what you want to hear?"

"I want to hear you say you're going to soak the wound every day, give him the antibiotics four times a day, and bring him back Monday. You don't, we'll call Public Health."

"You don't have to talk to me like I was some doper or dumb whore. Booker's my kid." She cocked her head at the examining room, ordering him into action with her gesture.

In return for treating her son, it would only be fair that he be allowed to hit her just once, right in that smug "I know I've got you" face. Right on her shit-eating grin, Webb thought, as he entered the examining room where Ray already had Booker positioned on the table.

"You and your bright ideas," he said to Ray.

"Just hold still and I'll try not to hurt you," he said to Booker, who pulled his head away and gripped Ray's hand tightly each time Webb approached. "Promise."

Booker looked at his mother, who stood in the doorway. "You hold still and you can sleep in my bed tonight," Mrs. DeJohnette said.

Booker bravely held out his cheek, his lips tightly pressed together. Webb cleaned the wound with hydrogen peroxide and covered it with Bacitracin ointment and a four-by-four gauze dressing. Booker struggled briefly, then allowed Webb to open his mouth and inspect the inner cheek. "All done," Webb said, lowering Booker from the table. His fingers fit comfortably into the grooves between Booker's ribs.

He wrote out a prescription for Ampicillin and gave her a brown envelope of samples. "If there's a temperature or more swelling, he has to be treated in the hospital."

Ray handed Booker a small paper cup of water; the boy winced as he swallowed the first of his pills. Then he tugged at his mother's shiny short jacket. JOURNEY was embroidered on the back of the jacket and there was a halo of grease on the collar; matching circles rimmed the pockets. Webb squatted down, eye level with Booker.

"You're going to be just fine. Your mom's going to take good care of you." Webb offered his hand. Booker held onto his mother's coat with both hands. "See you Monday. Right?"

The boy looked at his mother, and then nodded.

"You like sports cars?" Webb asked.

The boy started to smile but was stopped by his pain.

"You come back Monday and we'll take a quick ride in my MG. With the top down. Okay?" he said to Mrs. DeJohnette.

"Shake the man's hand," Mrs. DeJohnette said. She gripped the nape of his neck tightly. Booker held out his hand tentatively. Webb took it, feeling the small fingers squeeze, then draw back.

"You're a good boy, aren't you?" Webb said.

Mrs. DeJohnette picked up the wall telephone and dialed for a cab. When she hung up the phone, she headed for the door. Webb offered her two seats in the waiting room, but she took Booker by the arm and dragged him outside. They stood by the curb, Booker occasionally turning to look back at the clinic, Mrs. DeJohnette facing the beach and the ocean beyond. Only when she was in the cab, the door closed, did she turn to look sideways, a brief glance toward Webb, who watched from the waiting room.

"What are you going to do for my headache?" The jittery woman wore a faded cotton robe and red high heels. Webb checked his watch; it was nearly 4:00 A.M. "It's been going on for a week. Night and day. I can't sleep. I've lost five pounds. It feels like my brain is going to burst." The woman's words were staccato, rapid as bullets. She fanned her face with the lapel of her robe.

"Any cold, fever, symptoms of the flu? Any numbness, tingling, weakness, dizziness?" Webb was only going through the formalities. He wondered how long it would be before she asked for drugs.

"Dizziness. I stand up, it feels like I'm going to faint. Sometimes the room gets dark. My ears buzz."

"Any recent stress?"

"Honey, my whole life is stress. But I've had my worries before and never had these headaches. Never, never." The woman moved her hands jerkily toward her face, as though about to brush away an invisible spider. Webb guessed amphetamines.

"Never had similar headaches?"

"Never took an aspirin in my life. Don't believe in them. I wouldn't have come tonight, except I can't sleep, what with my head pounding. You got something, anything?"

Ninety seconds. The woman had shown admirable self-restraint.

"How about Darvon and a shot of Benadryl to get you to sleep?"

"Doesn't work."

"You've taken Darvon before?"

"Not in a long time. The last doctor stopped them with some kind of shot; I think it was Percodan or Demerol."

"We have a rule against dispensing narcotics." The woman's eyes were wet; she dabbed at them with her thumb. Maybe she was legitimate. He could give her a few Percodan.

The woman sensed her opportunity. "Please, just this once." She reached forward and squeezed Webb's hand for emphasis. Earlier it had been Booker's fingers. And in another time it had been Elizabeth's intertwined fingers on airplane takeoffs.

Maybe if she hadn't begged. If she had shown some strength. If he could have believed her. But no. Her hand was too practiced, insinuating itself into his.

"If we made exceptions, then it wouldn't be a rule any more. Too many people come just for drugs. I'm very sorry,"

Webb said. "Why don't you take a couple Benadryl and try to sleep it off?"

She was the third patient on his shift to ask for narcotics: two headaches and one backache. Almost invariably they came during the hours the bars were closed. Some angered him, others seemed pitiful, others might have a real headache. It was impossible to tell. There had been a time when he would have tried to distinguish motivation. Not now. A single rule for all was the easiest; he did not have to worry about getting into medical negotiations. A firm "No" closed the subject, sealed him off from manipulation.

Except for Booker. But that was the mother.

The woman snatched her hand from his, wrapped her robe around her, pulled open the front door, and tried to slam it as she left. The door eased closed, restricted by the vacuum hinge. The woman hit the glass with her fist.

"You could have given her some Tylenol with codeine," Ray said. He leaned up against the water cooler, his arm resting on top of the dispenser. "That wouldn't have been asking too much."

"So she could spread the word? You've got me in enough trouble already."

Webb looked out beyond the purple circle of light fronting the building. He could not see the surf, but envisioned the waves lapping against the beach. The water was constantly reshaping the coastline, coastal time measured in the hollowing out of cliffs and inlets and the rise and fall of the sand dunes that he took for granted. Time made visible by its effect. The woman measured time by the elapsed moments between desire and gratification; she had only been able to wait ninety seconds.

At quarter to five, Angel Williams stepped through the front door. He walked up to Webb and ran his finger along Webb's lapel. "Not bad, but the collar should be crisper. Remember, the graveyard shift has to stand out against the night. These people have bad dreams, they want the doctor to smell of rubbing alcohol, remind them of something familiar. Professionalism is nothing more than the impression of order. And you," he said to Ray, "you're going to have to do something about your hair. Try Selsun, or Head and Shoulders. Look sparkling. Radiant. Effervescent. Not like some clerk at a Goodwill dropoff."

Ray stiffened but said nothing. Williams continued. "The central switchboard received a complaint. Some woman said that you refused to treat her headache."

"A junkie," Ray said, looking at Webb.

"How'd you handle it?" Williams asked Webb.

"I offered her Benadryl and Darvon."

"No, I mean, what did you say to her?"

"You mean verbatim? Hell, I haven't any idea."

"This time of night the bogeyman gets a grip on the temples. Patients won't take no for an answer. Right?" Williams stared at the two of them, before pulling a packet of brochures from his jacket pocket. "The Instantcare Headache Clinic. I've hired a neurologist, one afternoon a week, over at the San Bernardino branch. We're going to offer a complete neuro exam, plus acupuncture and biofeedback as a basic package. EEG and group therapy will be extra."

Webb shifted uncomfortably.

"Two birds with one stone. You give everyone a brochure and a packet of four Tylenol with half-grain codeine.

Enough to get them through the night. Then, if they're legit, they can phone for the workup. If they're not, if they're just after drugs, you've handled them gracefully. No one feels insulted. Now isn't that easier than fumbling around, not even remembering what you told them, or what you're going to say next?"

"Williams, you are a genius," Webb said.

Williams tapped the side of his head. "Just a shrewd observer. People get upset when you don't know what to say to them. Say a mechanic opens the hood of your car. Which would you rather have him say: 'Let's see. It must be here somewhere' or 'It's a leaky gasket.'"

He dropped a stack of headache clinic brochures on a table in the waiting room and left some more at the registration desk. He turned and walked back through the examining rooms and the lab area, inspecting. "Good, everything's nice and tidy. You boys keep up the good work." And he was gone, out into the night that was just short of delivering up daytime.

Ray shook his head. "Not exactly what you expected when you went into medicine?"

"Life isn't exactly what I expected."

"That Angel doesn't miss a trick," Ray continued. "He's reduced everything to simple black and white. And, you know, he's right. Reduce the solutions to the possible. Like shooting a few nuclear scientists. Intimidation. Make the others scared to go to work. All those wimps with their fancy equations, make them shake in their Hush Puppies."

"The one-man-can-change-history theory has fallen into disrepute. I have it from irrefutable sources." Webb smiled, hoping that Ray would, too. But he didn't. He was ready to continue ranting. A patient appeared. Webb felt a sense of relief. Something to do, someone to treat. But he was wrong. It was another headache.

"You must learn to relax," Webb said. The middle-aged man held his head in his hands. Webb wished the man had a laceration or a sprained ankle, something concrete that could be resolved with sutures or a splint. He turned to the man's wife, a short, stocky woman who stood defiantly, her hands on her hips, and gave her the packet of four Tylenol with codeine. "He needs a full workup."

"He's had these headaches twenty years," the wife said, her voice shrill and demanding. "We've been to the best: Scripps, Mayo's, even Mass General. We know all about you doctors. What he needs is relief, not to have someone tell him it's all in his head." She did all the talking, her husband occasionally looking up at her; otherwise he remained focused on his hands or the sheet of the examining table. She turned to her husband. "Tell him. Tell him how much it hurts. Go on, don't just sit there. Tell him how much you're suffering."

She reached out and smoothed down a flap of upturned collar on her husband's jacket. Then she folded her arms across her chest. The man looked up as though to speak, but instead he rubbed his forehead and massaged his temples with his thumb and index finger.

"I don't know what else to offer," Webb said. "Headaches are tough to treat, worse to have." He put his arm around the man's shoulder, not sure of his own sincerity, wishing it were different. But he was tired and the man's passivity grated. He stuck the brochure in the man's hand. "There's nothing more I can do."

"Aren't you going to at least examine him? Maybe there's something wrong." The woman's face was round yet hawklike, like a well-fed bird of prey. Her head moved forward from the shoulders, darting and biting at the space in front of her. Webb had seen cockfights in Ensenada. Her husband had been mortally wounded long ago, but in some strange dance of ambivalence, his wife would blow a breath of life into him each time he was down, waiting until he was up again before resuming her attack. The curious thing was that she seemed genuinely worried and concerned about him, as though afraid she might lose her favorite sparring partner.

Webb dutifully went through the motions. He picked up an ophthalmoscope and looked in the man's eyes. Webb reminded himself that he was looking at the man's retina, not his soul. Up close the parts seemed normal. At a distance, as Webb put the ophthalmoscope back on the instrument tray, he could perceive the red blur of sadness that covered all that the man saw. He tapped, testing the man's reflexes. His arms, then his legs, responded appropriately, little kicks against the hammer. The exam was a waste of time. The man could see it in Webb's eyes. Webb could see it in the man's eyes. The man wanted to use the hammer on his wife, but he never would. When Webb finished the exam, he stood for a moment, directly in front of the man, and grasped his hands. They were cold and lifeless.

"Okay. Tell me what helps. What do you normally take?"

The man was wrapped in his protective blanket of pain. The man just looked at him, then at his wife.

"You're the doctor," his wife interrupted.

He patted the man on the hand. "Take the codeine and try to get some sleep," he said.

"Come on, dear," the wife said, tugging his sleeve. And she shot Webb the look that he knew was coming, the combination of hatred and defiance. "Whenever you guys don't know something, or can't do anything, it's in the head. Well, we're not paying for this visit. Not a cent. You didn't do anything. Send me to collection, see if we care." She took the headache clinic pamphlet from her husband, crumpled it in a ball, and threw it in the sink. "I wouldn't wish my husband's headaches on my worst enemy, not even on you, Dr. Smith."

Her husband wiped his brow as she spoke. He did not look at Webb. Together they trundled out the door.

Webb jotted down a few notes in the patient's chart. A few minutes ago he had resolved to be more charitable, more compassionate. He had tried, but compassion was not a role to be performed. They saw through him. Son of a bitch, they would be saying to each other. That's not true, he wanted to shout after them.

9

"**Y**ou bring the suntan lotion?" Joe lay in the back seat of the rented Mustang convertible, his head propped up with orange pillows Jessica had taken from his bedroom. He wore Air Force reflecting sunglasses and balanced an unopened Bud on his chest.

Coltrane soared through speakers on both doors; Jessica had brought a black leatherette medical bag filled with tapes. Her bare feet kept time on the dash. In her lap a small white cat lay, sound asleep. She had found the cat scratching at her front door screen the night before. She fed the cat a saucer of milk and a can of tuna. The cat spent the rest of the night restlessly sleeping inside the piano while Jessica dreamed of John Cage and Cecil Taylor. In the morning she named it Hip Cat.

Jessica turned to face Joe. "Think you should wear a hat?"

"Better to have a natural tan than mortician's makeup. Besides, the sun feels good."

Webb looked over at Jessica's satchel of tapes. "Where'd you get the bag?"

"Traded favors with a medical student."

"What did he get?"

"I bought the bag at a thrift store. A buck for a dream."

"No medical student?"

"Which would you prefer?"

"Déjà vu," Joe interrupted. "Last time I was in Vegas was on my honeymoon with Mary. It was her fourth and my third. The open highway and constant nattering."

"I get the point," Webb said.

"What a honeymoon. From the Hall of Justice until we checked in at Caesar's we kept asking each other why we'd done it. Neither of us had much of a track record. Then it was the big round bed and two days humping under the overhead mirror . . . until Mary pleaded for mercy. We went to the fights over at the Showboat, a bunch of welterweights throwing a hundred punches a minute. The stink of sweat made Mary all hot again and we did it in the men's bathroom just outside the showroom. I still remember her wiping herself with the paper towels from the dispenser." Joe smiled weakly and closed his eyes.

"You sure it was your wife that pleaded for mercy?" Jessica laughed and brushed a strand of hair from Joe's forehead.

They pulled out of the L.A. basin and onto the flat open desert. Looking east Webb could see no smog. A few streaks of cloud floated in the clean sky. It was a balmy early fall day and Webb felt glad to be alive. He had gone to bed directly after clinic. Four hours sleep and he was wide awake. Though he had not thought about it in detail, he had the sense that something wonderful might happen. What it was, he had no idea. He watched Jessica's feet dancing on the dash. Careful, Webb reminded himself. Don't spend all your joy in one place.

It had been such a long time.

He pushed the car up to ninety, the onrushing wind drowning out a McCoy Tyner solo. Jessica held onto her Dodgers' baseball cap, then spun it backwards, the bill hanging down over the back of her neck. The ruler-straight road flew by. It was the first time Webb had been out of town since his suspension. He tapped his fingers on the wheel.

At eighty-seven the car vibrated slightly. At eight-five and eighty-nine the vibration disappeared. Webb adjusted the speed, moving in and out of the gentle shimmy. Each machine has its own resonant frequency, a particular speed that causes the parts to hum. So do men. You just have to find the right speed. He took the car up to a hundred; there were no vibrations. Eighty-seven was the designated number.

"If we're going to get killed, why not save it until after I've broken the bank?" Joe's voice was already tired.

Webb slowed and considered turning back.

"Not on your life," Joe said, as though reading Webb's mind.

"What are you going to do with all the winnings?" Webb asked. "Buy a motel?"

"That's your trouble—always planning ahead," Joe said. The three of them laughed. The cat jumped into the back seat where it sat on the transmission hump. It cocked its head and looked quizzically at each of them in turn. They passed a highway patrolman; Webb slowed to sixty-five. He felt restrained, harnessed, like a thoroughbred forced to walk the track. There was more power underfoot, power in reserve.

Webb watched the officer become tinier and tinier in the rearview mirror. The speedometer crept up to seventy, seventy-five. Webb rolled down the window and stuck his face out into the wind. "Fuck it, I feel like living," he said into the roar, again lowering his foot on the accelerator.

Monotonous desert was soon punctuated and then dominated by giant rock formations. Peaks were jagged and barren; the sinuous carvings of former streams and the level delineation of various strata were plain to see.

They pulled into a roadside café: Red's Recovery Room. Webb and Jessica went inside for some coffee. Joe remained behind, resting in the car.

Jessica played with her slice of apple pie, picking up the corner of the crust with her fork, then mashing it down again. She raised her cup of coffee to her lips, then set it back on the saucer.

Webb ate in silence. There was nothing he could say. He watched Jessica toy with her food. He'd been glad when she'd said she'd come. On an outing like this one, three would have to be better company than two—so long as Jessica held together.

"We shouldn't leave him alone any longer," Jessica said. She still had not eaten any pie. Webb paid, leaving a larger-than-usual tip, and they walked back to the car.

Joe was motionless, his head propped up on the pillows. He was staring out across the road at a deep canyon bound by high sheer sandstone walls. Tears ran down both cheeks; the cat was licking them off his neck. As Webb stepped back, trying not to be heard, Joe wiped his eyes. "Nice view," Joe said, swallowing several times. Webb leaned over the folded-up convertible top and kissed Joe on the cheek.

"I never even gave it my best shot," Joe said, his eyes

focused on the horizon. "All bullshit and excuses. Don't make the same mistake."

"Yeah, it's a nice view. Like you could see forever," Webb said softly.

"I think we'd better get going. This Mustang wasn't built for my skinny ass. I'll have bedsores before we even hit the hookers."

"Joe. I'm sorry I didn't have you over when Elizabeth and I were together."

"Shit, it'd have been horrible."

"I just wanted you to know."

"Who's to say I would have come?"

"That's my boy." Webb gave Joe a light pat on the shoulder. "Come on, Jessica. The kid wants to hit the tables."

"You guys okay?" she said as she stepped forward.

The two men nodded.

Jessica opened the passenger door and slipped into her seat, Webb into his. They buckled up, backed up, and were off.

They took two adjacent rooms at Caesar's Palace. The bell-man unlocked the door between the two rooms, creating a mini-suite. Joe took the room with the two queen-size beds. He sat on the edge of the nearest one, wistfully looking at the other. The cat jumped from Jessica's large shoulder bag and claimed the second bed, perching directly atop one pillow.

"Maybe this'll be my lucky trip," Joe said to Jessica.

She was hanging up his clothes: two white dress shirts and a pair of gray slacks. She put his underwear and socks in the top dresser drawer. The other drawers remained empty.

"I prefer traveling light," Joe said.

Jessica helped ease him backwards into bed. Within moments he was fast asleep. Jessica closed the door gently behind her.

"What if he doesn't win?" Webb asked Jessica as he stared out the window at the gigantic round pool down below. It was late afternoon; the pool was crowded with sun worshippers in chaise longues.

"If there is any justice in this world, Joe will win."

"Like I said," Webb said.

Jessica frowned. "Please," she whispered, her eyes closed. "Please." She walked up behind Webb, rubbed her thumb along Webb's forehead. "It'll work out. It has to. Come on. We're on vacation." She stepped back and slid out of her jeans, then pulled back the covers of the giant king-size bed. "Last one in is a rotten egg." She waved at the overhead mirror.

Joe slept; Jessica and Webb went downstairs for an early dinner. Even at 5:00 P.M. there was a line. While they were waiting to be seated, the Incomparable Ralph—a short, wiry, high-strung man in his early twenties—did a series of card tricks. Webb watched with disbelief as the cards flowed from sleeves, pockets, supposedly empty wooden boxes. Webb asked him to go more slowly. Even at half-speed, there were no seams in his performance.

"You ever deal here?" Webb kidded.

"Me? Never." He clapped his hands together, then held them up, palms outward. "I'm just a simple magician eking out an honest living." An ace of spades appeared in his right hand. "Besides, in my spare time I'm studying to be a doctor." The king of spades appeared in his other hand. He dropped the two cards on his small portable performing table. "Blackjack." The small crowd laughed and applauded. Ralph tipped his hat. The ace of spades now was resting on his blond hair. And then, so was the king of spades. The table was empty. Again he clapped his hands, showed his palms. The cards disappeared.

He tipped his hat—there were no cards underneath—and walked off through the employees' entrance to the kitchen.

Webb waited as Joe steadied himself, adjusted his collar to partially conceal his skinny neck, aligned his coat and sleeve cuffs just so. They started toward the casino. His gait was slow and methodical; he paused and leaned against the front window of a men's boutique. The owner looked out at him, smiling tentatively, uncertain whether he might be a potential customer. Joe waved him away and set out again, Webb holding him lightly by one elbow, the way one might offer support to a proud elderly person. A portly woman in a full-length mink bumped into Joe just as they rounded the corner between the men's store and the side entrance to the main casino. Joe stumbled and caught himself, his outstretched hand flush against the store window. "Watch where you're going," the woman said, storming off. Joe regained his balance; a full imprint of his hand was visible on the glass. "Sorry," he mouthed to the man inside the store.

It was early Friday evening; the tables were just beginning to fill up. Joe took a seat at the nearest table and plunked down two dollars. Without looking at Joe, the dealer, a woman in her early thirties, tapped on the plastic Five Dollar Minimum sign. "You got any two-dollar tables?" Joe asked.

"Not on the weekend. Maybe daytime tomorrow. Check with the pit boss." Joe looked over at the man in the gray-tinted glasses.

"What do you think?" he said to Webb. "At five-dollar increments, we can only make eight bets before we run into the thousand-dollar limit."

"Why don't you try the two-dollar tables first and see how they're running?"

"We'd have to go to another casino. I don't know if I could make it."

"We could take a cab. Imperial Palace and the Golden Slipper are only blocks away."

Joe paused and scanned the casino. Approaching was a handsome man in a fresh linen shirt and blue blazer. Clinging to his arm was a statuesque, high-cheeked woman wearing a dress with a low neckline. A blazing diamond-and-emerald beetle dangled between her breasts, suspended by a thin gold chain. "You think they got that at the Golden Slipper? Not on your life," Joe said. He sat down on the stool and pulled out a hundred dollar bill. "Fives, please," he said to the dealer, who slid him a stack of twenty red chips.

For the first half hour the cards broke even. At one point Joe was up thirty dollars, at another he was down fifteen. Then Joe hit an icy patch. He lost four hands in a row. He pulled out another hundred, bet eighty, lost, pulled out two hundred dollars more, bet one-sixty and lost again. "That's six in a row, dealer. I hope you don't plan on making this a career."

She smiled apologetically at him but said nothing. Two other players at the table were actually winning. One man had had three blackjacks in the same period that Joe had lost six hands.

143

"I need more money," Joe said to Webb. "The next bet's three-twenty." He motioned to the dealer to hold the cards.

"You sure you don't want to bet a little less? Right now she's beating you like a drum."

"You got to stick with the system."

Webb pulled the remainder of the first thousand out of his pocket. Joe placed three-twenty in the box in front of him. A king and a six. The dealer had a ten showing. Joe sneaked a peek at the small plastic card that outlined basic play. "We're supposed to hit," Joe said. "But I have a feeling she's got a six under there and is going to bust. I stand pat."

The dealer stuck the corner of her ten under the other card and flipped it over: a jack. She swept Joe's chips into her tray. She looked at Joe, waiting to see if he wanted another hand.

"Deal around me, just this hand," he said. He turned to Webb. "I need six-forty for the next bet."

Webb shook his head. "We're here for the weekend. You get unlucky on Friday night and we're gone by tomorrow's checkout. Come on, let's get a drink and talk about old times."

"To hell with old times. We came to break the bank, not reminisce. Give me the rest." He held out his hand.

"Bet the three-forty you have left from the first thousand."

"Six-forty. The cards are bound to change."

"Try three-forty. If you win, then we're only down three hundred. If you lose, we play again later. Okay?" Webb gripped Joe by both shoulders, giving him a few seconds of firm massage. "Get in there, soldier, and show them what you can do."

Joe bet three-forty and hit a blackjack, getting back five-ten. He was only down one hundred and thirty dollars. "I told you we should've bet more. We'd be ahead if you weren't so cautious."

"Hindsight."

"Give me the money."

"Play with the nine hundred, then let's see."

Joe broke even on the first session. He was exhausted after an hour but played for two. Webb helped him outside for some fresh air. It was a warm evening. The brightest of the stars were settling into place for the night. The two men circled the pool where three young women were swimming laps of breast stroke. The women laughed and chatted as they glided effortlessly through the water. Joe slumped in a blue-and-white plastic chair.

"One more losing hand and the thousand would've been gone," Webb said.

"Since when have you been so chickenshit? Man, it's only money. You lose, you earn some more."

"Easy for you to say. Listen, this is borrowed money."

"What's the big deal? Angel Williams isn't exactly some folk hero. You need to, you stiff him."

"I can't, I need the job."

"Yeah, I can see your point. I guess I'm a little excited. I've always been a two-to-five, place or show man. Twenty or thirty bucks in an afternoon at the track and I'm hot shit. You know, I almost peed in my pants when I hit that five hundred dollar blackjack."

"We'll play again when you're rested." Webb watched the women finish their laps and climb the ladder out of the pool. The pool boy positioned their chairs to catch what was left of a sun rapidly sinking behind the mountains to the west. The women were attractive in their brief swimsuits. Webb would have slept with any of them. Yet he found them annoying; perhaps it was the condescending way they tipped the pool boy.

"What's your pick?" Joe asked.

"They'll all do. But I don't think they're our type."

"That's because you're spoken for. I could deal with any of them. Or all of them." Joe rubbed his hands together slowly. He leaned forward in the low-slung chair, but the angle was too severe and he couldn't position himself for proper leverage. With a hand on Joe's belt and another under his armpit, Webb was able to right Joe's center of gravity and give a boost to his falling quadriceps. Joe's shirt was damp. He exhaled forcefully, letting out a low groan as he rose. Webb gave Joe a little shove in the direction of the women.

"Good evening," Joe said, addressing the three of them, but particularly the buxom brunette nearest him. Her oiled chest glimmered in the light of the setting sun. Two of the women smiled. The third remained undecided, peering at Joe over deep pink-tinted glasses. "Here for the weekend?" Joe continued. The women looked at each other, then at Joe, who looked gaunt but dapper in his starched white shirt and gray slacks. His height was in his favor; he could have been a marathon runner on holiday. In the deepening shadows his jaundice was not apparent. The brunette patted an empty seat next to her and indicated that Joe sit. Webb retreated to the far end of the pool, where he could not listen. He was fatigued from the drive and was glad to have a few moments of quiet. Also, he did not want to witness what he presumed would ultimately be Joe's rejection. Women like that toyed with you, then waited around for Mr. Perfect, that is, until they reached their early thirties. Then they weighed possibilities. These women were young, probably no older than Jessica. For them Friday night in Vegas was bound to be a smorgasbord, and Joe did not look like prime rib. Webb rested his head on the back of the chair and dozed off.

When he awakened it was dark. There were several couples strolling around the pool, but Joe and the women were gone. He tried to imagine Joe taking on all three at once—as he had in Ensenada. First it had been the cockfights, Joe an acknowledged expert. Then it was the women, Joe lining up three teenage girls on the edge of a bed, their legs high in the air. Joe had gone from one to the other, like a robotic arm in a pastry factory, madly filling cream puffs. He walked down the steps of the whorehouse and faked collapsing in the street, laughing and beating his fists on the broken concrete. Two days later he was dribbling green pus. "I guess they got the last laugh." For two weeks his shorts stuck to him.

A slight breeze stirred; Webb went inside. On the way past the buffet line he stopped and changed two twenty dollar bills into silver dollars. He liked the weight in his hand, there was the sense of substance, a time when money had its own value. He dropped three silver dollars in the slot. Three sevens appeared and the bells went off. He didn't even know how much he'd won. An assistant casino manager appeared and gave him thirteen hundred dollars. Webb tucked the bills in his left front pants pocket rather than in his wallet. He would not mention the money to Joe. He would keep it in reserve.

Upstairs Jessica was trying on new canvas boots painted with roses and studded with small rhinestones. "They were On Sale, half off." She was not wearing anything else. She stood in front of the three-piece mirror folding out from the

147

fake French armoire next to the wet bar, one hand in front of her breasts, the other covering her pubic region.

"Once I played cocktail piano at Bloomingdale's. They put me between the Christmas tree and the down escalator and told me to play 'middle of the road.' I told them I'd never heard that song, but I'd learn it. The fruitcake manager giggled and thought I was adorable. My first gig, playing 'Melancholy Baby' to the Christmas rush while dreaming of buying the pair of hot, black leather boots on display at the base of the tree. But the boots were more than I made in a week."

"There must be ten thousand pianists in New York City," Webb said, propping himself up in bed, his legs dangling over the side. There was a dull ache at the base of his spine from sitting in the soft poolside chair. He put both hands in the arch of his back and pressed against the sore muscles.

"To a block. You had to audition to play for auditions. If you were lucky, you could land a job playing the same tune fifty times a day while a string of hopefuls danced their hearts out, five minutes at a time. I played the theaters for half a year. Sometimes they didn't even heat the building. You'd play in an overcoat, scarf, and gloves with the fingertips cut out— like some character from Dickens." Jessica shivered and ran her hands over her body as if fighting off the cold.

"And you loved every minute of it."

"Like rotgut wine, New York. Like a bad habit. Too long in that city and you end up eating the big soot sandwich. No thanks. California may be just another gigantic outpatient clinic, but at least there's more space between disappointments. Of course I miss New York every day I'm not there, but that's not enough to make me go back. Not until they're ready for me." Jessica sat down on a yellow velour-covered chair at the foot of their bed. She looked into the mirror, held up both arms in a mimicry of driving. "If I can steer my way through the minefields while I'm waiting."

She made a sharp turn to the left and fell off the chair. "Baby bumped herself on her future," she said, laughing, rising, and collapsing alongside Webb. There was the sharp reek of bourbon. Webb knew that some of the boutiques in Las Vegas served drinks while you shopped. Webb preferred to believe that she had not been drinking downstairs at one of the dimly-lit bars strung along the pathway between gambling areas. He wanted to believe that her drinking was part of her image of rebellious youth, not a need.

"I think it's time for a nap," Webb said. Jessica was already halfway under the covers. "But first let's get these off." Webb kneeled alongside the bed and pulled. The boots slid off easily. Webb held Jessica's calves, stroking their smoothness. He lifted her legs onto the bed, held them up while he pulled the blanket from under her, eased her back down and covered her with the turquoise hotel blanket. He caught his reflection in the overhead circular mirror.

"Just a little snooze before we break the bank," Jessica murmured, her arm over her eyes.

Before turning out the light, Webb checked Joe's room; it was empty except for the sleeping cat. He thought of bringing the cat in with them but decided that Joe might want some undemanding company when he returned. He returned to bed, laying on top of the covers, still dressed, his side against Jessica's blanketed back, and pretended he was raising a precocious child.

Webb awakened to the sound of retching. Next door, Joe was vomiting into a plastic ice bucket balanced on his chest.

The sound was horrible, magnified by the cone shape of the bucket; the smell was worse. Webb soaked a face towel in cold water and held it to Joe's brow, and then to the back of his neck. The six o'clock news was playing quietly on the TV.

Joe took the damp towel and wiped his face. "One margarita, hold the salt." He released his grip on the bucket and Webb took it into the bathroom where, without looking, he flushed the contents down the toilet. He rinsed the bucket and put it on the floor between the two beds.

"Just in case."

"I had her right here," Joe said, pointing to the palm of his hand. "She lives in Marina del Rey. Gave me her address and phone number."

"Did she know you were sick?"

"No. I didn't barf until the elevator, after I'd left her."

"Elevator? Here at Caesar's?" Webb started to laugh. Joe smiled weakly.

"No one ever said I was the perfect guest." Joe started to laugh but caught himself. He was hiccupping.

"And the woman from Marina del Rey? Good news to report?"

"Some things are private." He wiped his mouth and winked at Webb. "But I'd give her a ten. We're going to get together when I get back."

"And this weekend?"

"Can't. She's up here with her boyfriend. But she assures me it's nothing serious." Joe rested his hand on his abdomen. There was a slight bulge that Webb had not noticed before. Fluid accumulation. He looked away.

"What now?" he asked.

"A Compazine and a Percodan. We'll hit the tables when the room quits rocking. Say around eight." Webb took a vial from the cluster of medications atop the TV. He handed Joe one yellow Percodan, snapped the plastic lid back on, and put the pills on the edge of the night stand nearest Joe. He was pleased that he was not tempted.

Joe lost four hundred during his next session. He only lasted an hour, until 9:00 P.M., before caving in. He slumped back on one of the huge leather couches across the lobby from Check In. Within moments he was still, his mouth open, his hands folded over his now clearly swollen abdomen. It had been a stupid idea bringing him to Vegas, Webb thought, looking around as if for a nurse to take over Joe's care. He explained to the bell captain, who was eyeing them with suspicion, that his friend was not feeling well, but that he should be okay in a few minutes.

"He's not exactly good for business, so try to make it short," the bell captain said, holding out his hand. Webb slipped him five dollars. "Take your time," the bell captain said, as though they had rented the couch.

Webb waited patiently but Joe slept on, occasionally snoring. The bell captain continued watching them from his baggage checkstand. Registering guests standing in line for their room assignments stared at them. He hated their smugness. While one woman eyed Joe, a man and his wife shoved past her to the front of the line. What if Joe should die right here in the lobby? Webb thought. He was embarrassed for Joe. Sickness is so humiliating.

A young girl from Registration approached. "Could I help?" she asked.

Webb was relieved that the girl spoke matter-of-factly. "Do you have a wheelchair handy?"

"Sure." Moments later she returned and helped Webb get Joe positioned. The girl bent down and put his feet on the metal plates. "Normally there's a deposit, but you look trustworthy. Bring it back when you're through with it." She went back to registering a group from Omaha.

Webb wheeled Joe by Registration, leaned over and offered the girl five dollars. She waved him away. "Hope your friend is better soon," she said.

"**I**t's a good thing we're leaving in the morning," Webb said to Jessica. He was watching the evening news while she slipped into a black dress. "I don't think he's going to last much longer."

"What about his breaking the bank? We can't take him home without a last shot at the tables." Jessica pulled on her new boots and then sat on a chair, slumped forward, her arms hanging limply in front of her. "When the kids go to Disneyland, they get to shoot the shit with Mickey Mouse. All Joe has done is puke in his room and sleep in the lobby. He's not exactly going out in style."

"What can we do? I'd hate to have him lose what little money we've brought. Using his system, even if it were to work, which it rarely does, it would take days to make a real score."

"Well, it's too late to be practical. We need to think of something miraculous. How about having that magician Ralph deal him a few magical hands or paying the casino to let him win? It wouldn't cost them anything. Go on, try it. Give them a ring."

"That's ridiculous. They're not in the business of giving

money away." But he phoned anyway, reaching the casino representative in charge of promotions.

"Sorry, but we don't want people seeing how easy it would be to be cheated. We don't want Ralph anywhere near the casino."

"How about bringing a table to the room?"

"Can't do that either. Gaming regulations. But we can comp you for dinner at the Bacchanale room."

"My friend can't eat solids."

"I don't know what else Caesar's can offer. Perhaps he'd be better off at home. Anyway, Caesar's wishes you the best while you're here."

Webb put down the phone. "No dice."

Joe slept until 6:00 A.M. Then he knocked on the door separating their rooms. He wanted to play. Webb said it was a crazy hour, told him to go back to sleep, and learn some respect for others. He was dressing as he spoke. They were at the tables by quarter to seven. Surprisingly, there was still plenty of action, especially at the craps table. People in their Saturday night best, ties undone, trying to make up losses or prolong winning streaks.

Joe took a seat at a blackjack table, to the left of a middle-aged man and his young companion. They were playing twenty-five dollar chips but seemed to be more interested in each other. They sat facing each other, looking at their cards almost as afterthoughts. Webb stood directly behind Joe. He ordered himself a Bloody Mary. Joe passed on drinks. Joe took fifteen hundred in chips and played five and ten dollar bets. He stayed close to even for about half an hour.

Webb could see that Joe was getting tired and put his hand in the small of Joe's back, to brace him.

"I don't think the system is going to be the ticket. It'll take too long. I think I'll just bet it all on one hand," Joe said.

Joe abruptly shoved all of his chips into the square in front of him, before Webb could stop him. The couple next to him still looked dreamily at each other, laughing and giggling, as the dealer dealt the first card to each of them. Joe had the ace of spades. "Come on, ten," he said to Webb. The dealer dealt quickly, the cards flying, face up. She started dealing the second row when the lights flickered. The whole casino became momentarily dim, then black, and then the lights came on again. The darkness couldn't have lasted more than one or two seconds. Just before the lights came back on, Webb saw Joe switch his second card with one of the cards of the man to his right. It happened in a split second, Joe moving his hands over each other as though indicating that he didn't want another card. The other man noticed nothing, still absorbed with his girl-friend. The dealer also saw nothing, having turned her head to look at the pit boss.

"Blackjack," Joe said. He laughed and clapped his hands. "Fifteen hundred and it's blackjack."

The dealer lazily pushed Joe twenty-two hundred and fifty dollars in chips. "Must have been some sort of power shortage."

"If you ask me, I'd call it a power surge," Joe said. "I think I've had enough. Could you please help me cash out?"

The dealer called for the pit boss, who stacked Joe's chips in two wooden racks, then escorted him to the cashier's cage. Joe took the money, paid back Webb, then gave the dealer twenty-five dollars. "Remember me on my next trip," Joe said.

"Nice trick," Webb said as they waited for the elevator.

"Yeah. I saw the ten coming off the deck. Then my five. Just as the lights faded. Pretty quick, don't you think?"

Webb nodded.

"Besides, there's nothing better than making your own luck if you get the chance."

On the way back to L.A. they heard on the radio that there had been an underground nuclear test that morning in the desert just north of Las Vegas. Several townspeople were quoted as saying they felt the tremors. Most commented on a brief power shortage. Several hundred anti-nuclear demonstrators were arrested at the site.

"I guess I had an atomic blackjack," Joe said from beneath his new Panama hat, which shielded his face from the morning sun. "Sort of like radiation therapy for bad cards."

"What are you going to do with the money?" Jessica asked. They were cruising at seventy.

"Go to a cancer clinic in Mexico."

"What?" Webb said.

"You got a better suggestion? Maybe I should save it in order to finish college or buy an electric wheelchair?"

"They're hustlers," Webb said. "You know it, too."

"Maybe the blackjack was a sign. I figure that if an atomic blast can deal me a blackjack, those quacks might have some new treatment."

"And you expect me to drive you down there?"

"You can have all my margaritas."

"Which clinic?"

"The one in Tijuana that Steve McQueen went to."

"How did he do?" Webb said.

"It's my winnings."

"It's a bunch of bullshit," Webb said. He turned the radio to a station playing vintage Beatles tunes and stared out at the desert sliding by. The old Joe would have thrown away his money on a busted-down nag that couldn't even make it out of the starting gate before he'd give one of those quacks a cent.

"I'm with you," Jessica said to Joe. "Mr. Poor Sport's just jealous because he didn't hit the blackjack."

Jessica reached over and hit Webb on the head with her baseball hat. It was hard enough to hurt. She glared at him. She turned off the radio, flipped on her tape cassette. Benny Goodman's 1938 rendition of "Sing, Sing, Sing" crackled through the cheap cassette speaker. Joe pulled his hat down further over his face and tapped his foot against the back of the front seat. Jessica imitated Goodman, running her fingers up and down an imaginary clarinet. When Krupa's drum solo came, she pointed to Webb, who tapped on the steering wheel and obliged by making top hat sounds, his mouth in synch with the music instead of his thoughts.

"Yeah," Webb said after the music had softened his mood. "I could stand another vacation. Mexico's just the ticket." He reached between the front seats and gripped Joe's skinny ankle. "Besides, who knows?"

He looked at Joe, who was snoring softly. He turned back to the highway, for a brief second trying to imagine if there really was such a thing as a miracle. The thought made him momentarily happy, the mere possibility. In the desert, no cars in sight, the air unnaturally clean, it almost seemed possible.

10

"**V**egas okay?" Ray asked. He was cleaning his back teeth with a toothpick, which he flipped into the wastebasket. "There's nothing worse than getting your teeth cleaned and having the hygienist say you haven't been flossing." He smiled, his teeth yellow with years of neglect, and offered Webb a cup of coffee. The clinic was quiet, the last patient had just dressed and left. Ray straightened up the examining table, tossing some bloody gauze pads in a metal wastebasket.

"I don't think my friend is going to last much longer." Webb told Ray the story of Joe's jackpot, but Ray was inattentive, preoccupied. As always, his opened briefcase revealed complete attention to detail, every pencil and eraser in its designated place, a dozen floppy disks perfectly aligned in their gray plexiglass pouch. In contrast, Ray's clothing looked more wrinkled than usual.

"There's another scheduled for next week. They say they'll stop, but they don't. It's the military-industrial complex;

those guys will never give up. The sons of bitches." Ray stood holding a bloodied scalpel; Webb had just finished removing a large metal splinter. The splinter, deeply imbedded, required an incision. Ray absent-mindedly flicked the edge of the scalpel with his finger. "Maybe there's no point in keeping track by computer. Maybe things are too far out of control." As he talked, he took a clean four-by-four gauze pad and cut it in two with the scalpel. There was a faint ripping sound and the soft sizzle of overhead fluorescence.

"Did they give any explanation of why the power failed in Las Vegas? Do you know?" Ray gripped the scalpel. "Do you?"

"Could have been coincidence, or an overriding of the circuits. How should I know?"

"That's just it. They explode a ten megaton bomb, right beneath your feet, the lights at Caesar's Palace shut off, and you say it could be coincidence."

"And you know what really happened?"

"Obviously it was a testing accident." Ray dropped the scalpel in the sink. There was a harsh metallic crack. He disappeared and returned with his scrapbook and showed it to Webb.

On April 10, 1986, at the nuclear weapons test site in Nevada, an underground weapons effect test, code-named Mighty Oak, somehow got out of control. It left dangerous levels of radiation in the underground test tunnel, and possibly destroyed some $20 million worth of test equipment.

Ray took back his scrapbook and held it under one arm. "That was four years ago. It took six months to make the news. If I were you, I'd get a Geiger counter and check the clothes you wore in Vegas." Ray put down his scrapbook and went upstairs.

Webb had his box of diplomas. Jessica had her sheet music. Ray had his scrapbook. Webb picked it up and flipped through the pages.

The first section was filled with articles on nuclear accidents: Russian, American, French. The second section, separated from the first by a neatly labeled cardboard insert, contained mainly photographs of the victims of Hiroshima and Nagasaki. There were several pictures of makeshift hospital wards with Japanese doctors tending to the burn victims. Webb stared at the succession of children's faces: charred, shredded, bubbling, and peeling. Napalm burned, phosphorus burned, radiation burned and continued to burn, carrying with it an even more dreadful sentence.

Webb closed the book and sat down on the same stool Ray had just vacated. The children's faces brought back the memories. The first time it had been a baby drowned in a bathtub. The mother was in the living room, screaming. The father stood alongside the toilet in the cramped bathroom, trying to get out of Webb's way as Webb bent over the blue-mottled child, giving mouth-to-mouth to the cold lifeless lips. Alongside the boy was a yellow rubber duck. Webb could taste the boy's death, hear his last breaths rushing out of the wailing mother.

Later it was children under trucks, pinned against errant cars, buses, burned beyond recognition. Stabbed. Shot. Maimed and beaten.

Eventually he developed reasonable defenses against adult catastrophes. With children it remained a succession of first times. Sometimes he felt responsible, as though he shared in collective guilt for allowing these children to die in flophouse fires, or at the hands of some maniac or momentarily neglectful parent. So many times he had vowed that one day he would be able to do more.

Webb looked down at his white doctor's smock and the Instantcare logo written over his breast pocket. He looked at the blood-tinged squares of gauze still in the sink. He had removed a splinter. He walked to the waiting room and took a seat next to the door, facing out through the large front window and watched the night progress. In the back were some gifts he had bought for Booker DeJohnette: a cowboy hat and a hand-held computer football game. But Booker had not come by. When he did, Webb vowed he would personally drive him to County. How could he let this go on? But what choice did he have? Not only would he lose this job, he'd jeopardize the possibility of ever getting back his license. He would wait a few more days. Maybe he wouldn't have to make this decision. Maybe the mother would bring the boy in. Or call.

And then it was morning, someone tapping him on the shoulder. Webb rose from his cramped position on the hard plastic chair. He had the feeling of being jerked into position, his strings pulled. He turned, expecting Ray. He was surprised to see Jessica sitting in the next chair, watching him.

"Have you been here long?" Webb asked. He tucked in his shirt and pulled up his socks. There was a metallic, used taste in his mouth.

"A few minutes. I was on my way to Oblivion and thought I'd see a hero in action. I guess I was a little late for the main healings." Jessica leaned over and gave Webb a kiss. She smelled of mint toothpaste and maybe a hint of scotch. Webb was not sure.

"Do anything exciting tonight?" she asked, her face now only inches from his.

"I took out a splinter."

"No lives saved?"

"A splinter a goddamn monkey could remove."

"Aren't we being cranky." Jessica moved to the door. "You know, there are younger, more optimistic fish in the pond."

"A nice sharp kick in the balls. Just what the doctor ordered. Come on. Let's take a walk. I'll feel better after I compare myself with what's washed up on the beach."

The beach was already filling up with early risers: fast walkers, joggers, strollers. Some ran with headphones, others carried weights. Speed and effort seemed at odds with the quiet grayness that hugged the shoreline. A fine mist clung to Webb's face. At most he had slept an hour or two. He must have been dreaming when Jessica awakened him; the landscape seemed clothed in secret meaning, alternative explanation.

They had only walked a half-block when a Yellow cab rounded the corner. Booker and his mother got out and started toward the clinic. Booker saw Webb down the street and gave a tiny wave. Webb and Jessica returned to Instantcare.

Booker's cheek was indurated. It looked as though the skin might break down. Mrs. DeJohnette swore that Booker was faithfully taking his pills. Webb cultured the wound, checking for a possible resistant organism.

"Does it still hurt as much?" Webb asked.

"You said you would take me for a car ride." Booker pulled himself up straight, his chest out. "Fast."

"You're absolutely right. It's okay with you?" he asked Mrs. DeJohnette.

She nodded. "Make sure he wears a seat belt. You never can be too careful." Was this sarcasm, Webb wondered. Probably not.

Webb jogged the three blocks home, came back in the MG. Jessica, Ray, Booker's mother and the first of the day crew watched as Webb lifted the little boy into the passenger seat, strapped him in, gunned the motor, and zipped off.

Booker's eyes alternated between the tachometer needle, the speedometer, and the passing buildings. He made rumbling car noises as Webb went through the gears. They took a short ride on the freeway, then crept back along Canal Street toward the clinic.

"Let me drive," Booker said.

"You have a license?"

"Do you?" Booker said.

"I've got dozens," Webb said.

"Then give me one."

"It doesn't work that way."

"Why not? I need one. You give me one."

"You sure you're only four-and-a-half?"

"Who says?"

"Your mom."

"I'm almost five." He looked at Webb, his eyes dancing, challenging. "I can drive."

"Your feet wouldn't reach the pedals."

"I'll stand."

Webb stopped and parked the car in front of an apartment complex. "Here. Move over. Stand right behind the wheel." Webb leaned back in his seat, making room for Booker. It was no great effort. The boy was so slight. "We'll rev up the motor together." Morning traffic was just beginning. Webb put the gearshift in neutral, saying, "Stand on my foot, that's right." The boy put all his weight onto Webb's right foot which rested on the accelerator.

The motor revved into the red zone.

"Hey. You'll blow this thing up."

Booker looked at him mischievously and pushed harder. A window of the nearest apartment opened. "What the fuck are you doing?" someone yelled.

Webb pulled at Booker's arms and lifted his foot. "Clearing my plugs," he said.

"Well, do it somewhere else!"

Booker pushed again, giving the man in the window a four cylinder raspberry.

"Cut that out!" the man cried.

Booker stuck his head out the window and cocked his fist. His face had a broad, asymmetric grin, the wounded side lagging. It hurt him to smile, but Booker was smiling.

"Fuck you, and fuck your kid!" the man hollered and slammed down the window. Webb lifted Booker back into his seat, fastened the seat belt, and sped off. Booker was beaming.

They parked down the street from the clinic. "You had breakfast yet?" Webb asked.

Booker shook his head.

Webb stopped at Milo's and got some doughnuts, a carton of milk, and some fresh orange juice. Webb and Booker sat at the curb, eating and drinking. Booker chewed slowly, with one side of his jaw. He swallowed even more carefully.

"Do you get enough to eat at home?" Webb asked after Booker had downed two glazed doughnuts.

Booker wiped his hands on his pants. He did not answer.

"Is everything okay at home?"

Booker snatched another doughnut from the bag, and jammed it in his mouth.

"Your mom. She treats you right?"

Tears welled in Booker's eyes, but he said nothing. He was sitting a foot away from Webb. He moved closer, looked out at the surf, and finished his milk.

"We've got to go back," Webb said. "Your mom will be waiting."

Booker shook his head. He stood up and started to run down the street, in the opposite direction from the clinic. Webb ran after him, and picked him up in his arms.

Booker wiggled until Webb put him down. He stood with one foot atop the other. "Let's go," he said. "My mom'll get mad."

While Mrs. DeJohnette telephoned for a cab, Webb went to the back room where he'd stored the presents. He came back and put a big black cowboy hat on Booker's head, fastening the string under his chin. He stopped and stared at the ugly wound. There was a good chance that it wouldn't heal, he knew. He ignored his concern, instead handing Booker the computer game. The mother had brought her child in to be treated; he'd done all he could.

"What do you say?" Mrs. DeJohnette asked Booker.

"Thank you." Booker shoved the paperback-sized game into his jacket pocket, adjusted the chin strap of his hat, and mugged. He made his fist into a gun, pointed it at Webb and said, "Bang, you're dead."

A minute later Booker and his mom were inside the cab, pulling away from Instantcare.

"You're positive you're a doctor?" Ray said. "And you worked at County? You could have fooled me."

"You want to take him home, don't you? Or somehow give him a new life." Jessica asked.

"If only it were that simple," Webb said.

Jessica and Webb walked back to Oblivion. Milo waved through the misty window. "Any chance you could make me a hamburger?" Webb asked.

"The grill's not hot yet. How about some sliced tomatoes?"

"Sounds good. Heavy on the vitamins. I understand they're good for strapping yourself onto the wagon."

"Good news," Milo said to Jessica. "I think the pianist on the evening shift is having a nervous breakdown. He mentioned that he was going to the outpatient clinic over at Brentwood. So if you could make it the next two nights— might be temporary, might be longer, but it would be a start. Eighty bucks a night, plus food. Three sets. Think you can manage?"

Jessica smiled, a forced, uncomfortable smile that Webb had not seen before. "I get to play some of my own compositions?"

"Standards first. New stuff after they get to know you," Milo said.

"A mixture," Jessica said. "If I'm going to fuck up, it's going to be some of my own material."

"Am I going to have trouble with you right from the start?" Milo put his finger on Jessica's nose.

"If you get a chance, make up a little sign and put it in the window." Jessica slipped her dark glasses back on, rose, and went to the piano. Soon she was lost in Birdland, the Five Spot, Village Vanguard, wherever her mind took her. Webb smiled, but there was no response. She looked out beyond Webb, without a hint of recognition.

Jessica frowned and replayed the same passage over and over. Webb walked to her side.

"You'll do fine." Webb sat alongside her on the piano bench, their bodies inches apart, not touching.

"What if they don't like me?" Her voice was barely audible. She was scared.

"Don't be ridiculous."

"What if it happens again?" Her eyes were wide.

"Just play the way you always do. You'll be a smash."

Jessica rocked back and forth on the bench, her hands grasped tightly between her thighs. Webb put his arm around her and held her steady. She was trembling, a fine vibration of fear humming its own tune. And Webb knew of the time of hospital gowns and paper slippers, endless institutional nights as scary as the darkest jungle. She was a patched-up soldier trying to carry on.

"I was hoping it would be different," Jessica said after a minute.

"You'd feel better if you could talk about it."

"There's nothing to talk about. It was a long time ago, and it's not going to happen again. No, it's not." She slipped on her dark glasses, turned from Webb and started to play again. "I'll be just fine," she said to herself. "Just fine." And she was gone again, off-limits, Webb seeing only himself in the reflection in her dark glasses.

He continued to sit at her side for several minutes, until she turned, and with a shaky smile, motioned him away.

He decided to ask Mrs. DeJohnette if he could take Booker to the San Diego Zoo.

After he got back from Mexico.

11

The clinic was situated on the crest of a low hill in a suburb just south of Tijuana. Standing in the circular driveway, the two men could see the brown, clotted downtown area, life compressed into a dusty dark smudge beneath an equally dark wafer of condensed air. The smog stopped at the coastline. Beyond, the silvery Pacific glistened in the mid-morning sun. Directly below the clinic was a well-groomed neighborhood with manicured lawns and stately trees obscuring the bigger estates.

"Well, let's get on with it," Joe said, squinting into the sun and looking at the city. His voice was tired, drained of the hard bite, intermittently indistinct.

"You don't have to go inside," Webb said. "We could hit the bars and catch the toreadors."

"We'll just take a look. If you think it's complete bullshit, just tell me. Or better yet, don't say anything." Joe showed his teeth in what started out as a smile but died on his face as a grimace of pain. He had already had two Percodan on the ride—the MG had lousy shocks and a broken passenger seat—the springs needed replacing. The Mexican roads hadn't helped. Not once had he complained. Joe walked with a stoop, his former oversized frame now folding in on itself. He had to rest several times going up the eight stairs leading to the front door of the clinic. Inside he slumped in a wooden chair in the registration office. The chair scraped on the Mexican tile, a low groan of defeat.

He was taken inside by an American doctor wearing a white lab coat and khaki pants. Webb offered to stay behind, but Joe insisted that he join them. The three of them entered a spacious consultation room; the large bay window over-looked the Pacific; the sill was sufficiently high to block out any view of downtown Tijuana. Dr. Ross outlined the pro-gram: a combination of detoxification and stimulation of the immune system. Webb and Ross were approximately the same age. The medical credentials on the wall indicated Ross was university trained. He spoke quietly, hands folded on his desk, adroitly countering arguments before Webb had a chance to raise them. "Of course none of our treat-ments has yet been shown to be statistically significant. But that's because we individualize our treatments. The resul-tant sample size is too small to allow us to draw definite conclusions. We insist that you understand that we are not selling any new advances. We're merely saying that we have had excellent results to date. The statistics won't be out for another ten years and we don't believe that it's justifiable to withhold treatment until the evidence is definite."

Webb could not tell if Ross was sincere or sensationally poised. He had been prepared to distrust and dislike any doctor who worked here. Ross was disarming. Maybe he actually thought he was helping. Con artistry was the confidence man's shot at creativity. But the greatest artistry of all was the conning of one's self.

"The whole treatment package is four thousand dollars, minimum, more if the therapy has to be more extensive. If you want to go ahead with the treatment, you can make arrangements with the receptionist." Ross rose and stood by the window, looking at the ocean, his long lab coat silhouetted against the shimmering water. It was all so perfectly orchestrated.

Ross started to lead them down the hall but stopped after a few steps. Joe was unsteady. Ross called for a nurse; she eased Joe into the wheelchair. Ross took the handles and guided Joe down the long corridor, showing him the facilities. He paused at each doorway, allowing time for Joe to look in at the patients undergoing massage or receiving physical therapy. The rooms were brightly colored, some with murals showing smiling faces, children with kites and balloons.

Some patients smiled or gave a weak wave when Dr. Ross passed. Webb recognized the look. They were trying to be good patients, hoping that politeness might give them an edge against their advancing diseases.

"Did you read the recent article on Interleukin 2?" Ross asked Webb as they walked by a darkened room, lit only by a single overhead light. A man lay on a bed, receiving IV fluids. A bottle of intravenous medication caught the light, standing out against the darkness, the liquid shimmering in the glass bottle as the ocean had in Ross's window.

"I understand the early successes haven't been duplicated," Webb said.

"Poor patient selection and faulty analysis. You know,

statistics can be very misleading. We think it's a great opportunity."

"I'm sure," Webb said.

"It's good to be skeptical, as long as you're not closed-minded." Ross wheeled Joe out into the solarium at the far end of the corridor. Several patients were taking the sun. "Let me leave you here. They don't mind your asking questions," Ross said. "It's better not to rush into any decision. We can talk again this afternoon. If you want lunch, there's a cafeteria in the other wing."

Joe had Webb help him from the wheelchair. He walked over to two men sitting side by side, next to a broad juniper tree. "You think the treatment's working?" Joe asked, getting directly to the point.

"I think so. I certainly feel better than before," a thin sallow man with red cheeks said. "The food's good. I've gained three pounds." He nudged his friend; they both smiled.

"You've had radiation, chemo, the works?" Joe asked.

"Sure, but I should have come here sooner, when I was in better shape so I could have taken full advantage of the treatment."

"Me too," the other man said. He spoke in a hoarse whisper. One side of his neck had been carved away. He wore a red scarf to conceal the hollowness above his clavicle. "They have activities: movies, a mariachi band Tuesday evenings, bingo. You feel like you're still alive. Not like those callous bastards at the university who told me there was nothing more that could be done. Like I was bothering them, interfering with their precious research. At least here you are the main event."

"How long have you been here?" Joe asked.

"Three months. My doctors only gave me six weeks." The man shifted in his chair. A feeding tube came into view: an orange rubber tube protruding from the man's pajamas. It lay coiled in his lap, the visible end clamped with a hemostat.

The other man nodded. He saw Joe frowning. "Listen, six weeks is six weeks."

"Have you seen any . . . ," Joe paused and scanned the two men's faces. He was careful not to offend. "Cures," he said finally.

"Hard to say. We haven't been here long enough. But Dr. Ross thinks they're on the verge of a breakthrough." The man with the feeding tube looked up at Joe. "Dr. Ross is a wonderful man."

"I'm sure he is," Joe said. The three men looked at each other without further conversation. Joe watched as the two men soaked up the sun. He stared at their puffy feet and at their slippers dangling idly, just grazing the well-tended lawn. One man's slippers were brand new, the soles un-scuffed. Joe stared at the man's feet, at the soles which hadn't yet been tested. He motioned to Webb who stepped forward and helped Joe walk the fifty yards back to the car.

"I don't think so."

When Webb got Joe to the car, Joe fell back into the seat with a groan. Webb was exhausted from his own effort. He remembered the weight lifter at the beach, collapsing un-der the beach record. Carrying Joe around was getting to be a real chore. He slid into the driver's seat. The wooden wheel was reassuringly warm from the sun.

"Ross didn't seem like such a bad guy. He's well-trained. Who knows. Maybe he's got something," Webb said.

"Don't bullshit me. You doctors are always promising

something you can't deliver. That Ross is so fucking smooth, I wouldn't let him sell me a loaf of bread. I like a man with doubts, the more the better."

"You sure about this?" Webb asked.

Joe turned away, looking out at the driveway. "The place gives me the willies. Everyone hanging on, waiting, counting the days. It's not home. Maybe it'd be different if I had someone staying with me, like Mary, even. But all I could see while that guy was talking was the nighttime. Sure everything's rosy in the sunshine. But the nighttime. I bet that's when the patients kick off. You'd hear everything, the moaning. No thanks." Joe stopped and wiped his forehead. He was short of breath from talking; muscles stood out at the side of his neck.

"Where to?" Webb asked.

"I don't feel like going back to L.A. There doesn't seem to be any point. Just lying there, waiting. Besides, I'm nothing more than dead weight. If only I could just walk out into the water and call it quits." Joe put his head back against the headrest. The angle of the sun accentuated his hollowed-out cheeks. Webb could see the vial of pills peeking out from Joe's pants pocket. A nurse wheeled a patient past the car. The patient looked at them with vacant, sad eyes.

"I've got an extra thirteen hundred on me." Before leaving Venice, Webb had taken the thirteen hundred dollar jackpot money and stuffed it in his pants pocket. They had his jackpot money and Joe's blackjack money.

"Use it to fix up your place. I can't stand that old run-down sofa another day."

"It doesn't bother me," Webb said.

"Then get some decent lighting."

"I like it the way it is."

"Then let's piss it away at the track."

"I told you it's not open today."

"Two blind men stumbling around in the dark, right?"

"Something like that," Webb said.

Joe put his hand on Webb's thigh and gave a gentle squeeze. Then he moved his hand to the gearshift knob. He idly moved the gearshift back and forth, between first and second. Then he dropped his hand into his lap. Within moments Joe was asleep, his head lolling on his shoulder.

Webb started the car. The engine coughed; it needed new plugs. As he backed up, he thought of Booker standing on his foot, revving the motor. He shifted into first, and shot down the driveway between the rows of cypress trees marking the entrance. He sped away from the clinic, driving quickly as if he had a destination. He turned left, followed a series of winding roads down to sea level, then to the ocean. He turned south, stopping when he reached Rosarita Beach. It was a long expanse of nearly deserted sand; there was only the Rosarita Beach Inn on the five-mile stretch of beach.

"Are we here yet?" Joe said. He rubbed his eyes. "Or is this still Mexico?"

"What did you expect, that I'd drive you all the way to heaven?"

"No need, there's a bus leaving every hour." Joe pushed the car door open, picked up each leg, using his hands for help, and tried to step from the car. He fell in the sand, face down. Webb ran around the car and helped him up. He brushed the sand from Joe's clothes. Joe steadied himself, took off his shoes and socks, and wiggled his toes in the warm, cream-colored sand. Webb took off his shoes and threw them behind the front seat. The two men inched their way toward the surf, which was low and respectful, barely breaking, just curling around their feet.

They walked a short distance in the wet sand. Joe looked back the way they'd come several times, watching the ocean slide in and wash away their footprints. He reached in his pocket and pulled out the vial of Percodan. He snapped the cap, took one, and looked down at the rest. "Is this enough?" Joe asked.

"More than enough." Webb put the cap back on the vial and shoved it back in Joe's pocket.

They came across a rusted beach chair half-buried in the sand. Webb pulled it out, wiped off some caked sand, and offered it to Joe. Webb walked a few yards further down the beach, leaving Joe lounging at the edge of the surf. He tried to think of an act that would resolve Joe the way a song finds its way back to the dominant chord. He could understand last rites—not as the receiver, but as the giver. Take this holy water and I shall feel completed, relieved, finished . . . Webb searched for the right word, but knew there was none. He went back to Joe.

"Did you bring Mary with you?" Joe asked. "You got Mary in the car?" His speech was slurred; his eyes seemed glazed. Webb realized that it was his fifth Percodan of the day. And it was only a little past noon.

They drove back to Tijuana and got a room at a fancy motel near the Fronton Jai Lai. While Joe slept, Webb spent the afternoon betting jai lai, losing fifty bucks but enjoying the yelling and the dark anonymity of the stands. He had a few Dos Equis, not a lot, just enough to oil the wheels of his wagon.

When he returned it was late and the front office was dark. So were most of the rooms. Only a single TV flickered from the last room in a long row of single-story units. Joe was awake, curled up along one edge of the bed. The room was lit only by two small candle-shaped lamps over the bed. There was a heavy wooden cross directly above Joe's head. Christ floated eerily in the faint light from the flame-shaped lamp bulbs. Painted blood dribbled down his feet.

"You think there's anything at all to the clinic?" Joe asked. But before Webb could answer, Joe shook his head. Within moments he was asleep again.

There was no point in taking him back, nor in calling an ambulance. Joe's breathing was adequate, though shallow. He was in limbo, neither here nor there. Webb went to the bathroom and got out his travel bag. In a zippered side pocket he kept an empty syringe and a vial of morphine. He had stored the morphine before they left, telling himself that he would use it if Joe's pain got bad enough.

He checked Joe's Percodan vial. He had taken all the pills, at least twelve, maybe more. It should have been enough. But Joe hung on, snoring, grunting, his breathing occasionally pausing, but always starting up again. Webb decided to wait. He put the syringe and the vial in the top drawer of the night stand between the two beds.

He stepped out into the chilly night air, closed the door behind him. Across the street the Fronton Jai Lai light switched off, the light's after-image hovering in the suddenly darker sky. The image faded, replaced by a dusty darkness. Webb walked to the corner. In the distance unmuffled cars carried on. A solitary dog ran by, stopped, sniffed, ran on again. The air was still, then there was a stirring of leaves and papers; cold air blew down the back of his neck and up his pant legs.

He smelled a combination of fried meat and flour. With

his eyes closed, there was no mistaking that he was in Mexico. The city had a lurking, stealthy quality. Shadows moved among even deeper shadows, fading into corners and alleyways. It was the backdrop of anxiety dreams, an entranceway into uncontrolled thoughts and long-forgotten ghosts and demons. On any street corner he might be attacked. Or there might be no one. Just crumpled papers, cigarette butts, and fallen leaves swirling in a dry silence.

Webb walked down the main thoroughfare fronting the jai lai pavilion. He made a mental note of his path. He did not read Spanish and had trouble remembering the street names. The store signs were dimly lit by the occasional street light and a feeble moon perched atop the Fronton Jai Lai. The words were not just Spanish; they were truly foreign, filled with the dreadful anxiety of incomprehensibility. It was the language of nightmare, billboards from another world. Webb had a great fear of dying in a foreign country, surrounded by strange people in a strange landscape. He tried to humor himself. Everywhere was foreign country. Everywhere the land was unfamiliar, the people spoke in alien tongues. It seemed true, but he did not believe it, not for a minute.

Back at the clinic Webb had seen the fear in Joe's eyes. He would have preferred dying at home, if he'd had one. Webb pulled his jacket around him as he made a wide circle around the pavilion. He would try to give Joe enough time to make his own fate.

At the back of the pavilion, a solitary figure was urinating on a ticket booth. He did not move as Webb passed at a distance. The man took his time; he was whistling. Finished, he headed off down the street, disappearing into a thicket of shadows and streets.

Webb passed a leather craft shop with its suffocating raw smell of cheap hides. Men worked here, passed a lifetime in a room no bigger than a cell. Cutting out soles of shoes that would be scuffed and worn away, discarded as junk. And yet the men might be proud of their work, content to circumscribe their lives to the tiny confines of their shop. In the front window was a collection of such discarded soles, presumably tomorrow's garbage, maybe a form of advertising. Others worked in similar cells—doctors, accountants, toll booth workers—in fact, most regular jobs occurred in rooms of small dimensions, lives measured in minute movements, the eternal migration of inches, between car and home and wherever you went when the car and home and shop weren't enough. Inches, feet, yards. Small numbers.

Webb walked the streets, alert to unexpected sounds. He traced the paths of cars passing down nearby streets and alleyways. An occasional person walked by, always on the other side of the street, head averted. Only children skipped and hopped on the street. Adults knew better. And there were no children out in the darkness.

He would always be afraid. Better to acknowledge it than run from it. So he was frightened. Well, he was walking the streets of some foreign, undoubtedly dangerous city. It was no big deal to be scared.

Webb walked until the roosters crowed. He wound his way back to the motel. The shops were still closed, though traffic had started up. The motel was completely darkened. Joe was as he had left him. He did not respond to Webb's gentle, then more insistent shaking. There was a foul smell in the room, a spot of red blood on the back of Joe's pants.

Webb pulled back Joe's eyelids; his eyes were soft and peaceful.

"Last chance," he said aloud. "You want it here or at home?" Joe farted but did not respond. "You positive?" Joe farted again. The blood stain on his pants widened. Webb reached in the night stand drawer and withdrew the syringe and a vial of morphine. He filled the syringe, and shot out the air bubbles, out of habit. He considered Joe's arm, but thought a leg vein would be less conspicuous. He pulled up the cuff of Joe's pants. He took his belt and tied it firmly around Joe's lower calf. A large vein popped up, just beside his ankle bone.

The injection only took seconds.

Webb walked outside and threw the syringe and vial down a sewer opening, the syringe catching on the grating before plunging into the blackness below. Back in the room he consulted the telephone book. *Mort*: an international syllable. He found a mortician that spoke English and was open for business. The mortician would be there within the half hour.

He took Joe's wallet and watch and put them in his suitcase. He saved only the identification papers, to show the mortician.

He opened a louvered window at the rear of the room. There was the same smell of fried food. A platoon of crickets chattered beneath the window, a patrol of birds sung overhead. The sun was not yet up, yet it was lighter. Webb watched through the slatted window. A baby cried from a nearby house, a light went on, a mother yelled, there was a general ruckus, which eventually died away, and the sound of the crickets returned.

Webb walked back into the room, leaned over Joe, and

kissed him on the forehead. He tried to clean up some of the mess before the mortician arrived.

"**N**o plastic bag. Promise."

"Si, señor. We are professionals. This is our lives." The mortician and his assistant carried Joe into an old Cadillac ambulance that had been repainted black. In the light from the motel room some of the red still showed on one of the fins. Back in the room, the mortician filled out papers. "We need a doctor's certificate for cause of death."

Webb pulled out his California license. "I know it's not good here, but I've taken care of him through his illness. It was cancer." Webb gave the man eight hundred dollars.

"We need someone local. Don't worry. We'll take care of it. You come to the mortuary late this afternoon. He should be ready."

The mortician stood up and shook Webb's hand. He handed him a business card and a separate receipt. Outside the hearse engine coughed and died. The assistant cranked the starter; the engine wheezed and started up. The assistant gunned the motor, a loud, unmuffled roar.

"He's always impatient." The mortician smiled, his gold-capped front tooth catching the amber brake light, a great, warm contented smile. The ambulance doors were closed. Joe could have been going to the hospital for an appendectomy, a tonsillectomy, a chest x-ray. Or a cremation.

The sound of the crickets did not return until the ambulance rounded the corner and disappeared from sight.

Webb packed his things, and Joe's, and paid for the room. The mortuary was on a dusty side street, not far from a cluster of sleazy night clubs. In the broad daylight the sordidness of the district showed. At the end of the block a little girl held up her skirt while she squatted and peed in the street. A few feet away a scraggly mutt tried to hump an equally emaciated dog. The mutt rose on its hind legs, gave a few aborted thrusts, and fell over sideways. The other dog trotted slowly away, without looking back. The girl pulled up her skirt and ran inside a barely upright shack.

The mortuary, with its black-and-white tile floor, smelled of disinfectant, formaldehyde, and flowers. The mortician arrived with another man, similar in appearance, who was wearing khaki pants and shirt, and a pilot's hat, the visor low over his brow.

"He'll fly the plane," the mortician said. "He's making the trip anyway, so it won't cost you much."

A short middle-aged woman appeared, holding a terra cotta urn. She balanced it in her hands, away from her chest.

"I think we're all set. If you want to pay the remainder." The mortician motioned to the pilot. Webb took his jackpot money out and paid them both, giving an extra twenty to the woman proffering Joe's ashes.

"You can go with him, if you want," the mortician said. "There's no extra charge. It's a beautiful day. You might want to see the coast from the air." The man smiled and pointed to the sky.

Webb felt light-headed. He thought he might faint. He turned toward the doorway to get some fresh air, but the heat and odor of the street overwhelmed him. "You'll have to excuse me," he said, sitting down on the front steps.

"Of course. He was your friend." The mortician motioned to the lady. She handed the urn to the pilot and disappeared down the hall. She returned with a bottle of Coke. She made a point of wiping the top with a clean napkin, then opening it in front of Webb. He took a sip, the bitter metallic taste mixing with the smell of formaldehyde and disinfectant and dust. He could not swallow. His hands were sweaty; he was not sure he could stand.

He waited a minute, then rose slowly, carefully, bracing himself against the doorjamb. "I think you might as well go on without me," he said to the pilot.

The pilot nodded and walked away. The mortician patted Webb on the back.

"Thanks for everything," Webb said. "You've done a very professional job." The man beamed and shook Webb's hand. Webb turned and left. Moments later he was back in his car. He looked over at the passenger seat, at Joe's few belongings: a pair of pants, a shirt, some underwear and socks. Webb leaned back against the headrest. After a few minutes the tears stopped. He started to dry his eyes with one of Joe's clean undershirts but used his hand instead.

He looked up. Children were playing in the street. They were laughing. Webb got out of his car, walked around to the passenger side, picked up Joe's clothes and carried them back to the mortuary. The woman answered the bell. She smiled and bowed when Webb gave her the clothing. At the far end of the corridor, Webb could see the pilot chatting with the mortician. Webb motioned to him.

"I think I'd like to go with you," Webb said.

Webb held the urn in his lap as the single engine Cessna taxied to takeoff. Webb was afraid. Even though the plane was clean and the instrument panel spotless, he doubted that the pilot bothered with proper maintenance. It would be smarter to have stayed behind, he thought, as the nose of the plane tilted upward and cleared a small clump of trees at the end of the runway. But he didn't want Joe alone with some stranger.

He didn't believe in religion. He didn't believe in God. But he also didn't believe in being all alone.

The pilot wore headphones and flew without speaking. Webb watched out the window as the brown shoreline gave way to a deep Pacific blue. They passed through a succession of wispy clouds until the sky was nothing but bright blue.

"Any time," the pilot said, turning to face Webb. "Just be sure to open the window first." He flashed a sly grin.

And Joe was floating over the Pacific, as invisible as his beginnings. Webb closed his eyes for the rest of the flight, imagining a prayer, the words at the tip of his tongue. Joe would have laughed at him. But Webb continued, in the posture of prayer, but silently, his hands together, fingers and thumbs opposed.

"Goodbye," he said finally, opening his eyes just as the plane touched down.

"Goodbye," said the pilot.

When Webb stepped down from the plane, he needed help. His legs were shaky. The pilot steadied him with a hand on his elbow.

"First time in a small plane," the pilot said.

"Yeah," Webb said.

A half hour later he was at the border, answering the questions of a customs agent.

"You bringing any food or drugs into the country?"

"No."

"Do you have anything of value to declare?"

"No. Nothing I need to declare."

The man waved him through.

Webb pulled on his dark glasses and accelerated. Within moments he was on the freeway again. The morning report said increasing clouds and bumper-to-bumper traffic. Webb did not mind. He had all day, or longer, to make it home.

12

The first few nights were slow. By the end of the week word had spread along the beach. The nights Jessica played, Oblivion was packed. A columnist from the *Los Angeles Times* had written two paragraphs. "Promising and authentic," were the words Jessica quoted, during intermission, while she sat with Webb at the bar.

"Authentic," Webb said. "That's in between original and true." Jessica laughed nervously. She had her hair pulled back in a bun. She was wearing purple slacks and a light lavender blouse. "You should be very pleased," Webb added.

"So far so good. I've even managed to sleep three hours a night." The strain was obvious. So was her pleasure that she was holding up. "Milo says the job may be permanent. He's giving the regular guy another three days. Says he owes it to him. Besides, he doesn't want union problems."

"This is union?"

"Including health benefits. The works. It's just like the Big

Apple. Fifty-second Street with white sand and organic corn chips." She looked down at her hands. "You really think I'm doing okay?"

"Look. You've already got the place standing room only. You've got them eating out of your hands."

"Audiences are fickle. This week they're appreciative; they want to give a break to a newcomer. A week later, you're old hat. Bring on the new girl. The one with the big tits."

"You've got big tits," Webb said. He looked down at her chest, then drew his finger under her chin. He leaned forward and kissed her lightly on the lips. There was a faint trace of perspiration. Webb wanted to hold her hand while she played.

"Well, here goes," she said, biting down on her lower lip. Just a flicker of fear, then she was composed, head held back as she returned to the piano. She gave a slight wave to two regulars at the bar, before launching into a medley of early Miles and Horace Garland. She sang Billie Holliday's "God Bless the Child." Without looking up, she announced that her next number was in memory of a friend. Joe Walker. It would be the Gerry Mulligan composition, "Blues for Strayhorn." She played pianissimo, so softly people stopped talking or even clinking their glasses. She offered the music without embellishment or arpeggio, single notes for the melody, barely audible chords forming a distant background.

Several times Webb had gone into the back room of his cottage and sat in the easy chair—Joe's chair. Webb sat and looked out the window and wondered what Joe had seen in the final weeks. Once Webb even napped in the bed, fitting himself into the gentle indentation Joe had left in the soft mattress. The house rattled and echoed. Webb found himself waiting to hear a cough or a groan from Joe's room. Webb had continued to sleep in the smaller front room, the closeness of the walls curiously comforting. The cottage was too big for one person now.

Near the end of the piece Jessica paused, looked up at Webb, and nodded slightly, without expression. When she finished, there was complete silence. Someone clapped. Others joined in. Several whistled.

"Joe Walker," she said again, staring into the piano. She began again, a slow waltz, which, after twelve bars, she syncopated by introducing a four-four bass line. In another twelve bars she was in full-stride boogie-woogie. The crowd was jumping. Milo was behind the register, keeping time on its ancient metal skin.

"She can really play," Ray said. Webb had not seen him enter. He was standing directly next to Webb, who had to crane his neck to see Ray's face. Webb could not recall having seen Ray at Oblivion before. He looked wired; he reeked of garlic and stale beer. Ray tugged at Webb's lapel. "You got a moment?"

"Someone drop the bomb?" Webb said.

"Got a bad news call from Mrs. DeJohnette. Booker's got a fever and she wanted to you to phone some pharmacy for more antibiotics. I told her to bring Booker by, but she said it wasn't possible. She sounded real squirrelly, probably all drugged up. Then she said to forget it, and hung up. Come on, I've got her address from patient registration."

"A house call?" Webb looked at Ray. "Yeah, you're serious. Oh, well, I guess once every ten years isn't too often."

"Tell Jessica I'll be back in an hour," he said to Milo. He blew her a kiss and started out the door. Ray followed, ducking under the door frame. They walked along the beach, toward the public parking lot next to the exercise area.

"When I was an intern they told me to make a house call on this young mother who had tested positive for syphilis. She lived on the third floor of a run-down apartment building. One room for herself and her two kids: an underfed three-year-old girl and a newborn, sleeping in a crib next to a banging radiator. I'm standing in the doorway, introducing myself, and the three-year-old starts calling me 'Daddy.'"

" 'She calls everyone Daddy,' the mother says." Webb paused. They reached Ray's car, a blue '75 Oldsmobile. One fender was covered with Bondo. The rear bumper was held on with bailing wire.

"Did you give her a shot, for the syphilis?"

"I told her to make an appointment for the clinic. But she never came."

"So? What next?"

"So my instructor contacted the Public Health Department and the Police. Eventually she was treated. The kids went to a foster home." There was the sound of surf, and a sliver of moon rising in the rapidly darkening sky.

"I grew up in a foster home," Ray said as he opened the car door. "It's the pits."

"At least you grew up," Webb replied.

They turned off at Lancaster, made another right, and followed a narrow poorly-lit street into a district of tire shops, abandoned service stations, and converted motels. An uncompleted freeway onramp darkened a chunk of sky. Ray pulled up to the curb and squinted at the street signs. They were hard to see.

He stepped out, walked to the corner to get a better look.

Two black men stood in the lit doorway of a liquor store with metal grillwork over the windows. They talked and pointed. Ray got back inside the car, locking the door behind him.

"They've got the welcome mat out for us. According to the street signs, Booker should be on the next block." Ray pointed to a two-story stucco building crouched in the shadow of the unfinished onramp.

"Want to walk?" Webb asked.

"I think we'd better park as close as we can," Ray said.

"Good thinking."

Ray pulled into a parking spot in the middle of the next block, between a battered Chevy pick-up and an ancient VW. On the rear bumper of the VW was the slogan, "Get Out of America."

"What if she won't let us in?" Ray asked. He locked his glove compartment, checked behind his seat to be sure there was nothing of value, nothing to tempt the neighborhood thieves.

Webb didn't answer. He took his black bag with him, but held it under his coat as he got out of the car to check the numbers on the buildings.

Once a motel, it was now cheap apartments. On the roof was a solitary metal frame for what had once been the motel neon sign. The outline of the metal supports pierced the sky; they suggested warfare, destruction, and abandonment. The nearest building was of similar construction. A parking lot separating them was filled with weeds and old cars, several on blocks. A single floodlight illuminated the first few rows of cars. They read peeling labels on mailboxes to find "DeJohnette": number sixteen, second floor rear.

Webb tripped over a tricycle left in front of the rickety

outside stairs to the second floor. He caught himself on the wooden banister. His hand stung; he had picked up some splinters. He tried to see but the light was too dim.

They heard the sounds of gunshots from a nearby TV, a baby crying, teenagers arguing, traffic from adjacent streets. They started down the outside covered walkway leading past the upper row of units. A couple sat eating dinner in the first unit. They were clearly visible through the open curtains and aluminum-sided window. The man put down his fork, rose from the table, and opened the door.

"You looking for someone?" The man's arms were huge, folded across his chest like a DO NOT DISTURB sign.

"Booker DeJohnette," Webb said. "I'm the doctor that's been treating him at the clinic." The man looked at Webb, at Ray, at the woman who had also stopped eating.

"Yeah?"

"We work for Instantcare, the clinic out at the beach," Ray said.

"You ought to work on the mother. She's the one needs help." The man slammed the door, returned to his meal, at the same time glaring out at them through the window.

"Maybe we should send for backup," Ray said. "Like in the movies."

They reached number sixteen. Webb knocked, then stepped back. Below them was the darkened parking lot. Beyond, the twin apartment building appeared like a reflection.

The door opened; it was secured by a chain. A disheveled man in his early thirties peered out. He was not wearing a shirt; on his chest was a tattooed spider web, the spider directly above his left nipple. Without a word, he closed the door.

Webb knocked again. The man pulled aside the window drape. Webb stared in, the man stared out. The door opened again, this time without the chain. The man's arm blocked the doorway.

"Hey, man, can't you see it's late? We're not open for business." He was Webb's height, but skinnier. His skin was a greasy yellow; he had a wisp of a goatee.

"I'm Booker's doctor. He hasn't been back to the clinic."

Webb looked into the room over the man's shoulder. It was furnished fifties motel style: two twin-sized beds, a night stand, and a set of dresser drawers. The beds were unmade. The rabbit-ears of the TV were bent and drooping.

"The kid's fine." The man started to close the door, but beneath his defiant manner was doubt. He stopped, shook his head and motioned to the door adjacent to the TV set. As Webb stepped forward, the man asked, "You're not cops?"

"No." Webb held his hands in front of him, palms upward. "Everything's cool."

"I never heard of a clinic doctor making house calls."

Me neither, Webb thought.

The man led them inside and opened the door to the adjacent room.

Mrs. DeJohnette sprawled on one of the beds. She looked up at Webb through half-closed lids. For the first time Webb saw bruises on her arms. They looked like skin pops. On one side of the bed was a wastebasket half-filled with Kleenex. A jar of Vaseline and a bottle of massage oil were heating under a goose-neck lamp curled down on itself. The door to the adjacent bathroom hung precariously by the lower hinge; a triangle of harsh fluorescent light poured into the room.

Booker was asleep on a cot jammed up against the front

window. He wore a leather-sleeved L.A. Dodgers jacket, and Keds. A thin blanket lay at his feet. In one hand he held a Ninja turtle doll. The computer game Webb had given him was at the foot of the bed.

The woman wore a silk nightgown, stained in front, and a tattered green plaid robe. "I'm all through for the day," she said, waving the two men away.

"It's me, Dr. Smith." Webb drew closer. "I want to take a look at Booker."

She rose up on one elbow. "He's sleeping."

"It'll just take a second," Webb said.

"No need. He's all better." Her speech was slurred.

"A quick exam and we'll be gone." Webb cautiously walked over to Booker. The boy's jaw was barely visible in the shadow of his jacket. Even so, a walnut-sized lump could be seen rising from his cheek, the skin shiny and tight around the mound of reddened skin. He leaned over to get a closer look. Booker mumbled and turned, but did not awaken. His breath smelled faintly of raw meat.

Booker's forehead and cheeks were blazing hot. "He must be 104," Webb said to Ray. He turned to Mrs. DeJohnette. "He needs surgery. His jaw's abcessed, and he's septic. There's no time to lose. I'm taking him to County." Webb shook the boy's shoulder. Booker murmured, opened an eye, looked at Webb, and closed his eyes again.

"Get the fuck out of here," the woman said. "Now."

"What did you give him?" Webb said. He bent over her, trying to hold her attention. "One of your pills?"

"It's no business of yours."

Webb reached over and picked up the bedside phone. "Give me the number of the Child Protective Services Agency," he said. He jotted down the number on a pad next to the phone. "Last chance." Webb pointed the receiver at Mrs. DeJohnette.

"Hang it up," she said.

"Come on, Dorothy," the man said from the doorway. "The kid's sick."

"He's not going anywhere." Mrs. DeJohnette reached under her pillow and pulled out a pistol. She aimed it in Webb's general direction.

Webb jumped back.

"Dorothy, put that thing down," the man said.

"Don't 'Dorothy' me. He's not your kid. Show 'em the door."

"At least I know what's good for him."

"Yeah, you're a real genius. That's why you hooked up with me. Get them out of here."

The man shrugged apologetically. "Okay, boys. You heard the lady."

"I didn't hear any lady." Ray stepped forward and lifted Booker from the cot. He cradled Booker in his arms. The boy opened his eyes and looked blankly at Ray.

"Put him down." The woman had her gun aimed at Ray's head.

Ray tucked the blanket gently under Booker's chin. "This is your kid's life we're talking about." He started edging his way toward the door to the other room.

"Put him down." There was a change in her voice. She was all business.

Ray walked toward the door. Webb stepped between Ray and Mrs. DeJohnette.

"Get out of my way," she said. She cradled the gun in her hands, her elbows supported on her inner thighs.

Webb tried not to look at the gun. "You can tell them at the hospital that you just came to town. No one has to know about the knife." Webb hoped she couldn't tell he was lying.

"You can't fool me," Mrs. DeJohnette said.

"He's going to die if you don't get him treated properly."

"Die?" It seemed to register now. The gun tilted downward, aimless.

Webb sat on the edge of the bed, his hands folded in his lap, the doctor at the bedside, comforting a sick patient. "The infection's serious. Judging by his temperature it's in the bloodstream, which makes his chances fifty-fifty."

"Bullshit." But there was a tentative ring to her voice.

"No, not bullshit. I've seen kids die from an abcess. Please be reasonable."

"They're right, Dorothy," the man said.

"Don't poke your nose in my business. Booker's not yours." She turned to Webb, her robe opening to her upper thigh. She made no attempt to cover herself. "I get Booker back. Swear it."

"I can't promise that."

Her voice trembled. "You sure that he's got to go? We can't try more pills?"

"We've already wasted too much time. At the hospital they'll take proper care of him. That I do promise."

"Me, I'm a two-bit whore. No county agency is going to give two loose shits about what I feel, what I want." She pointed the gun at Webb. "'Cause I've got scum on my hands doesn't mean I don't love Booker as much as any mother could. Don't think you know what's good for him and I don't. Yeah, *you* know all about Booker, you doc-in-a-box." She turned to Ray. "Put Booker back where you found him and get out of here."

"You're right, Mrs. DeJohnette," Webb said. "I can't kid

193

you and you can't kid me. But you can fool some over-worked and underpaid social worker. Tell her you don't know what happened, you left the kid with his old man, who split on you." Webb pointed to the bathroom. "Get yourself tidied up, put on some nice skirt and a long-sleeved blouse, and show up regularly to visit."

"No. Not County. They'll check my record."

"What about a private hospital?" Ray said to Webb. "You show up with a boy this sick, they can't just turn him away. How about a hospital where you have some pull?"

"I think I can guess what you have in mind." Webb said.

"Sure. Good Hope's only a couple miles from here. It's worth a try."

"They got social workers there, too," she said.

"You don't have a choice. You leave him here, he's going to die," Webb said.

"You really think I can get by them?" she asked as she put the gun down.

"Visit every day, sober and appreciative. Doctors like that. Plenty of gratitude. Maybe even bring in some cookies. Yeah, you make an effort and I'd say your chances are good."

"They take him, you'd better start running." Steel re-turned to her eyes, but there was a difference, a spark of possibility. How long it would last was another matter. Webb had seen the look a thousand times in the County clinic patients. Give someone a good pep talk and he'd buck up. A week later he'd be back with the DTs and a bag of excuses.

Webb bet a hundred to one against Mrs. DeJohnette fol-lowing through. But it was a bet he did not want to win. "Get dressed. But be quick about it."

Mrs. DeJohnette pulled herself to her feet. She moved

slowly toward Booker. She put her cheek up against his good cheek. "You'll be as good as new," she said. Then to Webb, "I won't be a moment."

Booker's arms clung to Ray's neck. He held his soiled doll limply in one hand, the other rubbing his eyes. He seemed vacant, as though not yet awake.

Webb crouched down. In the dim light the abcess looked even larger.

"Momma," the boy said.

"She's coming with us," Webb said.

"Momma loves me," Booker said.

"Sure she does," Webb said.

"Momma loves me," Booker said again.

13

"**W**e don't have insurance," Mrs. DeJohnette said to the intake clerk in the emergency room. "We're new in town, and I'm between jobs."

"I'm very sorry. We'll need some reasonable guarantee of payment." The clerk was a slender, effeminate man in his early thirties. The Larry King Show was playing on a small Sony Watchman guarded by four partially-filled styrofoam coffee cups on the man's desk.

"No sweat," Mrs. DeJohnette said. She reached into her purse and gave the man two one hundred dollar bills.

"We need a minimum of five hundred. If the charges are less, we'll return the difference. You have a credit card or a bankbook?"

"Can't you see how sick my son is?"

The man looked up from his papers and his TV, glancing at Booker for the first time. "Oh. Why didn't you say so, hon?" He took a closer look at Booker's swollen jaw. "That does look nasty. Maybe we can get you Medi-Cal. Take a seat while I make some calls."

Mrs. DeJohnette carried Booker to a long bench adjacent to the doors leading to the treatment area. Sitting on the bench reminded Webb of the wait for his hearing at the Medical Society.

It was a busy evening; prospective patients filled the seats and benches, several paced the small corridor. Webb and Ray walked to the Coke machine. Webb had mentioned his stint at Good Hope but not his dismissal from the staff. It would have been a lot safer for him at County. Once he was inside the treatment area here he was sure to be recognized.

Time passed. Yet everyone sat quietly in his place despite the fact that some were doubled over in pain. No wonder they were called "patients."

Ray kept checking his watch. In fifteen minutes their shift at Instantcare would begin.

"Why don't you go on?" Webb said. "I'll catch a cab as soon as Booker's squared away."

"You sure?"

"Sure I'm sure. Angel keeps telling us how many backups he's got standing in the wings. So he can get a fill-in for me if he has to."

Before leaving, Ray walked over to Booker and stroked his hand. The little boy barely stirred in his mother's arms.

An hour later the clerk still sat behind his desk signing in a stream of patients. There was no hint that they would ever be reached. Webb went over to him.

"You got Mrs. DeJohnette's paper work done yet?" Webb said.

"You a relative?"

"A friend."

"I've paged the social worker, but at this hour—she might have gone out for dinner."

"It's been more than an hour."

The man shrugged. "It's not a perfect system, but I'm doing the best I can."

"The boy is really sick. He needs to be seen by a doctor now."

"Please have a seat."

Webb checked Booker. His eyes were glassy and he was wringing wet.

"I thought you could do something." Mrs. DeJohnette spoke with mingled fear and anger. Webb was worried about her, too.

He stepped onto the rubber mat activating the sliding doors and entered the treatment area. There was a blast of chilled air, the smell of alcohol and disinfectant, the sounds of sickness and suffering. The stocky head nurse came forward, striding with the brusque efficiency of an NCO. Two steps and Webb was sure she spent her off-hours practicing tae kwan do. Webb recognized her face; he scanned her name tag surreptitiously.

"Miss Dawson."

"Dr. Smith," she responded. Then she started to say something more, but stopped. Webb could not remember any particular past encounter, but her sour countenance certainly hinted at a prior run-in. Had she forgotten his competence and was simply glad he'd been canned, pleased he had gotten his comeuppance? He could have been reading too much into the look of contempt this harried ER nurse had given him. Maybe he meant nothing to her.

Through the ER doors he could see Dorothy DeJohnette

making small jerky movements, one hand at her mouth, pulling at her lip. She wouldn't hold together much longer sitting, waiting, on that bench. And her son was by now in urgent need of medical help.

"I hate to barge in, but I need a favor. There's a boy in the waiting area who needs immediate attention. He's septic from a wound infection." Webb was unsure and so he spoke too loudly, too forcefully. This wasn't what he had intended.

"Your son?"

"No."

She scrutinized him carefully. "Wound infection? What kind?"

"I'm not sure," Webb lied. "His mother says that he fell on a pencil. But I do know he's got a huge abcess and is spiking a high fever while the intake clerk is farting around, shuffling forms."

"Let me take a look."

He followed her through the doors back to the waiting room. Webb pulled back the lapel of Booker's jacket while the nurse inspected the wound. "Okay bring him inside," she said to Mrs. DeJohnette. "Dr. Kimball is the pediatric surgery fellow on duty. He'll be with you as soon as he can." She started to walk off, then turned back to Webb. "This boy. He's a personal friend?"

"From the neighborhood."

"Oh." She frowned at Webb. It was as though she were inspecting him through an invisible microscope. It was the look he had received at the Medical Society hearing. It was the look on Detective Reynold's face and even, to some extent, Angel Williams's expression on hiring day. He both wanted and didn't want to know what she was thinking. It couldn't be good. Maybe she was just trying to figure out how someone could throw his practice down the drain, throw his life away.

Dawson still fixed him with her icy stare. He wasn't sure just what he was being accused of. Then she was called to start an IV on a patient going into surgery.

Mrs. DeJohnette tugged at Webb's sleeve. "He's getting worse."

"It'll just be a few minutes before a doctor sees him." Webb tried to sound reassuring, but his voice seemed gruff and distant. In former times he would have grabbed this Kimball by his arm, ripped him from what he was doing, and marched him over. He would have demanded, insisted, yelled, whatever it took. Now he hung back, intimidated, afraid of the consequences of making a scene.

It was late and he was tired. He tried to write his script, cobble together a story to tell, if the pediatric surgery fellow were to recognize that the wound had been partially treated and demand an explanation. He could just say that the boy and his mother were from his neighborhood. She refused to tell him where she'd gotten the antibiotics. This excuse seemed adequate; Webb didn't feel capable of a more extended deceit. In the busy emergency room a sentence should suffice.

The intake clerk approached. "Good news. You're all set for tomorrow. The social worker said she'd process your papers in the morning."

"What about tonight?" Mrs. DeJohnette demanded.

"The two hundred will cover your ER visit."

"No, that's not what I meant. I'm not leaving until my boy is fixed up." Her voice had risen; she was only moments from exploding.

"That's up to the doctors. If they feel it's a true emergency, there is a medical indigent program."

Webb expected Mrs. DeJohnette to tell the clerk off. But she didn't. Instead she hissed at Webb, "I thought you used to be a big shot here. You're a doctor. Do something."

Webb approached Miss Dawson who was taping down the IV tubing. Her back was turned.

"Which room is Dr. Kimball in? I'll get him myself."

"Don't start pushing me around," she said. "The treatment rooms are for staff only. You shouldn't even be in here."

"The boy's sick as hell."

"Dr. Kimball can decide that."

"*I've* decided that. Get Kimball now."

"Dr. Smith. Please sit down outside."

"I'll give you five minutes."

"You have no authority here now. So try to behave like a human being."

"Four minutes."

Kimball was new, Webb guessed, fresh out of his residency. He was perhaps five-six; he wore cowboy boots, a monogrammed lab coat, and a smug expression.

Ignoring Webb, Kimball asked Mrs. DeJohnette, "What seems to be the problem?"

She pointed to Booker's jaw as Kimball escorted them into the nearest empty treatment room. When Webb started to follow, Kimball told him to wait outside.

Webb stood on the threshold, watching, as Kimball examined Booker.

"No big deal," Kimball said to Mrs. DeJohnette. "Looks

like a dental abcess. We'll give him a little Ampicillin and have the oral surgeon take a look at him in the morning."

"What's his temperature?" Webb asked from the doorway.

"The nurse will get it."

"She already took it. It was 104 earlier, on arrival. It's probably 105 now. A lot higher than you get with an uncomplicated dental abcess."

"I've seen it plenty of times," Kimball said with an air of experience.

"Ampicillin isn't going to touch it," Webb informed him. "The abcess needs to be drained tonight. Look at the position. The infection may involve the carotid artery. He could have a stroke. You could lose him in a minute."

"If you're such an expert, how come you brought him to me?"

"He needs a good surgeon," Webb said.

Kimball handed a prescription to Mrs. DeJohnette. She took the slip of paper reluctantly. "You try him on the antibiotics," he told her. "In the morning, bring him to the dental outpatient clinic and get some x-rays taken. Have him take two baby aspirin every four hours." He put his hand on Mrs. DeJohnette's shoulder, indicating it was time for her to leave.

"Do you know what it's like to get sued for malpractice? Have you any idea how that can spoil your day?" Webb yelled at him. "Do yourself a favor. Phone the pediatric surgeon on call. Share the responsibility. Certainly, one call wouldn't be too much trouble."

Miss Dawson appeared in the doorway. "Gentlemen, please. There are other patients out here. I suppose I should have introduced you two. Dr. Webb Smith. Dr. Fred Kimball. Dr. Smith was on staff here, but he's—taken a leave of absence. Dr. Kimball, in my opinion, it wouldn't hurt to get Al Steirman's views. That's a pretty nasty infection."

The two men glared at each other. Neither extended his hand.

"Leave of absence?" Kimball smirked, but he thumbed through the staff directory. New doctors soon learned which nurses knew more than they did. Moments later he was describing Booker over the phone. Webb had had little contact with Steirman, but he'd heard good things about him. As far as Webb knew, Steirman was first-rate.

Then Kimball hung up. "Steirman said that you knew what you were talking about." He paused, then continued. "Suppose you show me what's worrying you."

Webb put his hand on the back of Booker's neck. It was fiery hot and damp. "Show the nice doctor your throat," he said as he directed the overhead examining light. Booker grimaced as he opened wide. "There, see the asymmetry between the two tonsillar pillars? The slight swelling on the left? That's classic for a retropharyngeal abcess. Antibiotics can't touch it."

Kimball peered closely. "Hmm. I'm not sure I see anything."

"By the time it's obvious, it's often too late. Please, trust me."

"And he got this way from falling on a pencil?" Kimball asked. "I find that hard to buy."

"I've seen others."

"What treatment has he already had?" Kimball asked.

"Two courses of Ampicillin."

"You know that?"

"That's what she told me."

"So you don't know if he actually got the Ampicillin?"

"He got it."

"But you can't know for sure. I'm still in favor of another course of antibiotics."

"Why don't you get Steirman back on the phone?"

"Why don't you tell me what really happened?"

So Webb did.

Twenty minutes later Booker was on his way to surgery. And Kimball hadn't even checked to see if Booker had insurance.

Kimball whistled as he lathered and rinsed. When finished he held his two arms aloft like some proud child. Without even noticing Webb, a scrub nurse swept into the room and pulled on Kimball's gloves. She left the room. The two men stood at the sink.

"You mind if I watch?" Webb asked.

"You're not on staff."

"No one would notice. Besides, I've been there before. Working around the carotid sheath can be tricky business."

Kimball looked around the otherwise empty scrub room, nodding at the stacks of scrub suits and gowns on the corner shelves. Moments later Webb was masked and gowned, complete with a cotton hood that covered all but his eyes. The nurse returned and gowned Kimball. She looked briefly at Webb but said nothing. Webb doubted that she would recognize him; he could have been a burglar or second-story man.

"He's a friend of Steirman," Kimball said to the anesthe-siologist, not bothering with names.

Booker was completely draped with the exception of his cheek and the left side of his neck. The skin at the angle of his jaw was tight and shiny. Under the harsh surgical light the swelling was less apparent. "It could be superficial," Kimball said to Webb.

Webb frowned but said nothing. He stood to the side, his unscrubbed hands clasped behind him.

Kimball made the opening incision. The tissue was bright red and inflamed, but there was no obvious single focus of infection. He stopped at a row of black dots just beneath the surface and pulled with the forceps. A series of sutures came into view. Surrounding each suture was a small amount of pus. Kimball turned to Webb, then back to the wound. He removed Webb's sutures, dropping one in a test tube, for culture. The rest went into a specimen bottle. His exploration of the subcutaneous tissues revealed nothing further. Then he widened the incision.

Careful of the lingual artery, Webb thought to himself.

There was a gush of blood. "Hemostat," Kimball yelled at the OR nurse. "Now."

"Yes, sir." The nurse slapped the instrument into his hand. With a single precise movement Kimball had the bleeding controlled. Webb was pleased to see that the man was quick with his hands but felt he should have been more cautious in exploring the wound.

Kimball tied off the bleeder, then probed further. From his position Webb had difficulty clearly seeing the carotid sheath. He would have identified and tagged the vessels before proceeding. But Kimball was using forceps and his finger to create a dissection plane.

"Slowly," Webb said quietly. "There can be anomolous branches from the jugular."

"I know," Kimball said. He took the handle of his scalpel and spread the two layers of tissue further apart. A reddish gray mass popped into view. Judging by the circumference of the dome, Webb guessed the abcess was the size of a golf ball. Which meant that it would be up against the carotid artery and the jugular vein.

"Don't pull," Webb said. "It could be adherent to the vessels."

"You want to do this?" Kimball snapped. The two men locked eyes. His voice softer now, Kimball asked, "What would you suggest?"

"Simple drainage. Even slight trauma to one of the branches can lead to retrograde occlusion. Particularly with the amount of inflammation that must be present."

Kimball stood with his hands resting on Booker's draped cheek. "Yeah."

He made a small incision in the dome of the abcess. All these years and it was still a smell that made Webb swallow hard. Kimball cultured the wound, then irrigated the abcess, first with saline, then with antibiotics. The abcess continued to drain and Kimball repeated the procedure. At last, satisfied, he turned to the nurse. "Penrose," he said.

Kimball fastened the drain into place with a single suture at the top edge of the incision. He packed the wound with iodoform gauze.

"You can lighten him now," Kimball said to the anesthetist. "We're almost done."

Webb excused himself. He dropped his mask, hood, and gown in a hamper just outside the operating room. It would be another twenty to thirty minutes before Booker was in recovery.

Mrs. DeJohnette sat in the family room outside the operating suite. Webb walked by her with a nod and went down to the deserted doctor's lounge. In the mornings this was the center of activity, upwards of fifty doctors jammed into this little room. At off-hours the lounge was usually empty, as it was tonight.

On the bulletin board were rows of notices of job opportunities including several for volunteer positions overseas. One was for a children's hospital in Morocco. Webb tore off the announcement and jammed it in his pocket. Then he sat down in the near darkness. The lounge was lit by stray shafts of light from the hospital rooms and nursing stations overhead. It was as though the sky was filled with cubicles of disease and injury.

The lounge was only four walls, a few couches and chairs, a dead TV, a coffee machine with a single red eye, a dozen half-empty coffee cups and a scattering of old newspapers and medical journals. Yet it had been home to generations of physicians, the single place in the hospital most likely to be missed by those who had retired. It was where stories were shared, where men strutted, laughed, worried, phoned families with good and bad news, and choked back tears.

In the beginning, Webb had joined in. Later he saw only individual faults and the all-pervading ugliness of a group of men that he had grown to despise. His mistake was now all too obvious. It had been himself he had hated the most.

He remembered the evenings when Elizabeth had waited for him in the lounge with a novel, while he was upstairs, operating.

Webb tried to envision Jessica sitting, waiting, greeting him when he got free, going out for a late meal . . . It wasn't imaginable.

It was Elizabeth he missed; Elizabeth he really wanted. Elizabeth had valued what had been best in him.

Webb closed his eyes and wondered if she might give him

another chance. The possibility gave him hope. He knew where she worked. He could camp outside her office. But he couldn't go to her with another investigation hanging over his head. Either Child Protective Services would investigate or the Medical Society would find out. Kimball clearly disliked him. Of course he would report him. Only four more months to wait for his license to be restored, and he had blown it. Again. He found it impossible to sit. He left the lounge and wandered through the hospital corridors.

Good Hope had one remaining closed-off ward that had not been renovated. Webb stopped in front of the deserted cavernous room. Moonlight sliced through the darkened ward, streaming onto buckling linoleum floors. Webb was reminded of an abandoned cathedral, of former times, before antibiotics, when ether was in vogue, when life had scale and order. When medicine had a certain medieval elegance.

And when Booker would have died.

He hated modern medicine's lack of grace. Now there was the new aesthetics of technology. But bedside manner would not have saved Booker.

When he returned to the surgical waiting room, Kimball was at the charting station talking to Mrs. DeJohnette. As he spoke, she nodded dutifully. When he finished, she shook his hand.

Kimball came over to Webb and suggested that they take a walk in the corridor.

"Don't say anything," he began. "Just listen. That boy had some pretty fancy suturing done on him. I don't know you, but I know good work when I see it." They were now halfway down the otherwise deserted corridor. "But you know that the law requires that I report any suspicion of child abuse or neglect. I'm guessing that an investigation of the mother

will lead back to you. And you only have a few months to go
to get your license back, right?"

Webb nodded.

"But the mother's a flake?"

Webb nodded again.

"I'm really sorry, but my first responsibility is to the boy."

"I know."

"I know you do. Mrs. DeJohnette told me how you tried to
help Booker. And she told me to leave you out of it."

"Are you going to report her?"

"What do you suggest? I can't ignore the situation and just
let the kid go home again."

Webb was silent. He looked out the window at the end of
the hall at the empty ambulance below.

"You do what you have to," Webb said. "I understand."

"You were right, of course. He had to be opened up. Tomorrow would have been too late." Kimball's admission
was not as grudging as Webb had anticipated. "When I saw
the pus right up against his carotid artery . . ." Webb had
the momentary pleasing sensation of being included as a
colleague, comparing reactions with an equal, quickly followed by a sinking feeling. He could appreciate now exactly
what he had lost.

The two men walked back to the recovery room. Mrs.
DeJohnette was at Booker's bedside watching drops cascade
down the IV tubing. The boy was asleep, his face a mass of
bandages. Webb looked at the vital sign clipboard at the end
of the bed. His temperature had already begun to fall.

Webb left the hospital by the rear entrance. A glance at his
watch showed him that his shift at Instantcare was nearly
over. He wondered what Angel Williams had said to Ray. But
he was too tired to care.

14

Williams was in his office at Instantcare when Webb arrived the next day. Angel was seated at his desk, the glow from the miniature clinic sign turning his bald head violet. He was adding up his receipts. As his stubby fingers punched in the numbers on the calculator, he grunted and swayed, Angel's version of the tango.

"I'm in the middle of a column. Hold on." Angel was gracious as ever.

"I'm history," Webb announced. "I think I have some back wages coming to me." That caught Williams' attention.

"What about two weeks' notice?"

Webb shrugged. He was relieved that Williams wasn't going to attempt to talk him into remaining with a lot of bullshit about profits and potential at Instantcare.

But Williams went on. "Its just as well. You've been under quota on 50 percent of your shifts. With some people, it's too hard to start from scratch and teach them how to practice medicine. I think you're one of them. You never really caught on. Don't worry, you can be replaced. Easily. In one day. You'll be gone and forgotten. Out of sight, out of mind. Easy come, easy go."

Webb was relieved to see that even as he spoke, Williams was writing a check. When Angel proffered it, he took it. Then he removed the stethoscope from his jacket pocket and draped it around Angel's neck.

"Here, listen to your heart," he said as he tugged on the rubber tubing. "I'll bet you don't hear a thing."

Within three days, Booker's fever was gone. Webb's wasn't. He waited for the phone to ring, the door to knock, the mailman to deliver a summons. He slept fitfully, his sleep riddled with nightmares. Instead of resorting to alcohol or Valium, he started running along the beach each morning, walking for miles in the evening. He felt better outside his cottage, away, somewhere where he could not be reached.

At his original hearing, when he might have made a reasonable case for his behavior, he had gone out of his way to be obnoxious. Now, when he wanted desperately to defend himself, he could find nothing he could say on his own behalf, even if he were given the chance. He had violated so many statutes that any explanation was irrelevant.

Jessica had come over one night after finishing at Oblivion. A nightclub in San Francisco had offered her a job, she said. She was unsure of what she should do. He had no advice to offer. He wouldn't urge her to go and he couldn't ask her to stay.

He visited Booker in the pediatrics ward at Good Hope.

He tried to find a clue to his own situation in the head nurse's manner of response when he asked about Booker's progress. But he couldn't read her. There was a social worker at the chart station who glanced briefly at Webb and then went back to her writing. He wondered at the significance of this.

When he reached the ward, Booker was not in his bed.

"He's down in X-ray getting a long bone, rib, and skull series," the pediatric ward nurse told him.

Bone surveys were standard when evaluating for child abuse. Evidence of broken ribs or limbs would buttress suspicion.

"He'll be back in a few minutes," she added matter of factly.

Webb excused himself politely. "I'll come back later."

He went to the visitor's cafeteria, selected a sandwich and tried to eat. But the bread was like sawdust to him. X-rays were the first step; the investigation had begun. He felt sick and lightheaded. He bolted from the cafeteria, not sure where to run. He stepped outside the hospital, but there was no place to go. He forced himself to return to the ward.

Kimball was at the charting station when Webb walked out of the elevator. "So far, so good," he said to Webb.

"X-rays clean?" Webb asked.

"As a whistle."

Webb was standing next to the children's drinking fountain. It came to his knees, which were shaky.

"How's he coming along?"

"He's doing fine. I've got him down for discharge tomorrow, if everything works out."

"The mother?"

"Oh, she's stuck by her story. She hasn't involved you. She's tough. But she has been spending time here. And Ann

Gelb, the social worker, has got her signed up for parenting classes at John Adams Community College. A public health nurse is scheduled to make home visits until Booker's completely well."

"And Protective Services?" Webb forced himself to ask.

"They decided there was insufficient cause for a formal inquiry."

Webb couldn't make himself ask the next question. Now it was all up to Kimball. Either he would inform on Webb to the Medical Society, or he wouldn't. Even when it meant the restoration of his license, Webb couldn't make himself beg.

15

The children's hospital was situated in the heart of the city, immediately adjacent to the medina. It had been built by the French government at the turn of the century. Once a general hospital, it was now primarily a center for reconstructive surgery for southern Morocco. The director, Assad Barka, had spent a portion of his training at L.A. County at the same time as Webb. Webb had explained about the suspension of his license. It might be restored soon, it might not. He did not want any misunderstanding.

Dr. Barka indicated that his surgical assistants were nurse practioners. Having a license was an unnecessary formality in a three hundred bed, fully-occupied hospital where the annual budget was a mere four million dollars. He had asked that Webb try to bring some extra suturing material, and any antibiotics that were not too outdated.

Webb had taken what he could from Instantcare.

"You familiar with Volkmann's contractures?" Dr. Barka

asked. They were standing outside one of the children's wards.

"From textbooks," Webb answered.

"We have four to do this week. A prominent healer in one of the High Atlas villages believes that you can treat pneumonia by tying a tourniquet around the forearm. Sometimes he leaves it on too long."

Dr. Barka started into the ward. It was long and narrow, and several of the beds had more than one child. Beyond, through the open window at the back of the room, was a small garden of palm and olive trees. Bougainvillea climbed the adobe wall at the back of the yard. There was the sound of cars honking, and the occasional braying of a donkey coming from the medina, and the smell of spices and incense.

The children looked up as the two doctors entered. Those that could, smiled. Dr. Barka leaned down and picked up a small boy of about seven and held him in his arms. "We guess he left the tourniquet on overnight." The boy's left hand and forearm were withered and contracted into a claw. The skin was pale and shiny, the subcutaneous tissue replaced with hard fibrous tissue.

"If we can relocate the extensor tendons, he can at least use the hand for gripping and carrying."

"Why doesn't someone talk to the man who did this?" Webb asked.

"We have. It doesn't make any difference. The mountain families believe in his powers, and so does he. It's like the polio vaccine. We give it out but not everyone takes it. Science means nothing to these people. In the summer we average about four cases of polio a week."

Dr. Barka looked at the boy and spoke in Arabic. The boy

nodded and held out his hand. Webb took it gently in his. Dr. Barka told Webb that he had explained. Webb was going to fix his hand.

"You told him that it wouldn't be as good as new?"

"That's not necessary. He knows you'll do the best you can."

Webb shook his head.

"You'll get used to it. It used to give me a chill. Sometimes it still does. The way they trust you."

Webb ran his fingers along the shiny hand and the atrophied muscles. The boy's hand would always be grossly deformed. He had the boy open and close his fingers. There was some residual strength. Perhaps he could make some modest improvements. He patted the boy on the head.

Barka looked out at the ward. "Club foot, spinal scoliosis from old polio, congenital deformities, cleft palates. There's enough work for an entire university surgical staff."

They continued down the ward, Barka introducing Webb to the children. "I heard that for a while you ran the orofacial anomaly clinic at USC."

"Not exactly. I worked there a half-day a week. When I wasn't too busy making money."

"We're glad you're here. Everyone here has their story. Most charity stems from a troubled heart."

"Charity?" Webb smiled. "You mean I'm not going to make three grand a procedure, cash in advance, you bill your own insurance company?"

"It was four grand in Paris," Barka said. The two men laughed.

The children smiled shyly. A couple said a few words in French. Others mumbled greetings that he could not understand. Some of them spoke Berber. There were so many, and some of the deformities were so severe. Webb knew the answer lay not with corrective surgery, but with public health: education, vaccination, proper use of antibiotics, and decent prenatal care. He was trying to repair what should have been prevented.

After lunch in the small, dimly lit cafeteria, Webb went to the operating suite. It was a series of six rooms separated by chest-high tile partitions. Dr. Barka had the nurse practitioners do the opening incisions, then he went from room to room, supervising and performing the technically difficult procedures.

Webb scrubbed, mesmerized by the flow of water down the rust-stained sink. Through the doorway he could see the yellow-stained tiles of the operating room with its iron IV poles and plain concrete floor. It was a far cry from high-tech Good Hope, but it was more inviting. As he scrubbed he hummed to himself. He was alone in a foreign land and it was all right.

A young, olive-skinned woman stood in the doorway. She wore a surgical scrub suit. She spoke in accented English. "You're from Los Angeles?"

Webb nodded.

"How long do you think you'll be staying?" she asked.

"I'm not sure."

"We're glad you could make it."

"You're from here?"

"A small town on the coast. But I live here now. Originally, I came for a week." She tucked her hair under her cap.

Webb dried and powdered his hands, and slipped on his gloves. He would write Elizabeth that evening. Better yet, he would phone. The sharp desert light pushed back the shadows, filling the room with the lovely heat of possibility.

An orderly went past, pushing an ancient gurney with frayed rubber wheels. He stopped at the doorway of the operating room, lifted the boy and placed him gently on the operating table. The nurse anesthetist took the boy's hand and whispered something to him. The boy nodded and closed his eyes. The woman administered the anesthetic. Minutes later Webb was on a stool in the operating room, cutting through the scarred tissue left by another healer who thought he was doing the right thing.

And piece by piece the scarred tissue came away in his hands.